PROJECT PARADISE

Spice Up Our Marriage Book 1

PHOEBE ALEXANDER

MOUNTAINS WANTED

Printed in the United States of America

First Printing, 2018

Mountains Wanted Publishing

Georgetown, DE 19947

www.MountainsWanted.com

Created with Vellum

To the ladies of The Juniper Court Series: Isabelle, Sylvie, Emme, Vicki, Jennifer and Lainie.

My husband accused me of not even trying to fit in.

We've been having this argument ever since we moved with our perfect 2.5 kids to Juniper Court, our new neighborhood in the suburban sprawl of Sunview. Well, only two kids, actually, as having .5 would be virtually impossible unless I were pregnant. And God knows I'd rather be poked in the eye with a sharp stick than ever be pregnant again.

But back to my story: David took me into his arms last night, pinning his eyes on mine with the most loving, husbandly look he could muster, and asked, "Valley, you know how much I adore you, but for my sake and the kids', could you at least *try* to make friends with the other moms in the neighborhood and at the kids' school?"

I discovered on the very first day of school last September when I went to pick up my darling angels— Aidan, age 10, and Aubrey, age 7—what the moms in Sunview are like. I mean, they're wearing the hell out of their yoga pants, that much is to be expected. They're scurrying about in their minivans and roomy but sporty SUVs with their hair in perfectly imperfect messy buns, all hyped up on caffeine from their Starbucks addiction. All of that is status quo.

What I wasn't expecting were the sideways glances at my raven black hair and the tattoo peeking out the top of my low-slung skinny jeans. I wasn't expecting the judgmental stares at my apparently inappropriate cleavage or the fact I drive a sleek black convertible Mustang. (Yes, the kids fit in the back just fine.) Oh, and let's not forget the multiple pairs of disparaging eyes glued to the stiletto-heeled black leather boots that come up past my knees.

I don't how all of these suburban moms can be such clones. It's like a cookie cutter came along and stamped them out one by one, with their blonde bayalage hair, staid French manicures, ridiculous designer handbags, and sensible flats. I'm sure if they looked way back into their pasts, they'd remember who they used to be before they had kids. Maybe they were artists or musicians, or had aspirations of curing cancer someday. I'm quite sure they had admirable life goals beyond their entire existences revolving around their kids 24/7.

Don't get me wrong. I *FLOVE* my kids. They are the most amazing two humans ever to emerge from a vagina. But I'm not just a mother. I have other interests, other pursuits and diversions. And I find it pretty pitiful that LuLaRoe and mocha Frappuccinos would be among a grown woman's most consuming passions.

Speaking of which, I might as well just tell you now: I hate coffee. Go on, boo, throw tomatoes, whatever. Not liking coffee around here is like a capital offense! But coffee is seriously the worst, and every time I hear one of those boring, vapid soccer moms go on a long-winded rant about the barista who screwed up their venti half-caff soy latte, I just about lose my shit.

"Couldn't you do something to get to know one or two of them? You know, try to establish some sort of rapport so our kids will get invited to birthday parties and such?" David questioned, his hazel eyes pleading with me.

I hate that he's unhappy with me. He wants to be the pillar of the community type who invites everyone's families over for BBQs and pool parties and all that. But it's just so not me. Boring small talk with a bunch of Stepford wives over a paper plate piled with hot dogs and potato salad is my worst nightmare. If I'm going to throw a party, I want it to be all adults, and I want it to actually be FUN!

But I do enjoy making my husband happy, in more ways than one (*wink*). So I asked gently, trying to rid my voice of any unintentional traces of sarcasm, "What do you suggest?"

"Doesn't the PTA sponsor a yoga class on Tuesday and Thursday mornings in the school gym? I bet you'd meet some nice ladies there."

I looked at my husband and sighed. "Honey, I don't know what to tell you. I just don't do Downward Dog. I'll be happy to turn over and do doggie style with you right now though!"

David just shook his head. He knew what he was getting himself into when he married me. I've never been one for conformity.

As previously mentioned, I love my kids.

There, I have to repeat that, lest you think I'm a bad mom. But for fuck's sake, why is it they have to argue over every single little thing? I swear they would argue about whether or not the sky is blue. I walked into the living room to find a full-on debate about which is better: tater tots or French fries.

My kids know better than to fight loud enough to disturb my time with my precious Kindle. Those smutty books I read are really the only escape I have from my monotonous job as chef, cleaning lady, and taxi service. Besides, I was getting to a really good scene...the hero and heroine were finally going to do it!

Sometimes I can't believe I have a college degree in interior design. I don't think I need a degree for arbitrating fights about processed potato products.

"What's going on in there?" my Mom voice boomed across the room as I stomped in. "You—over there!" I pointed to my son, directing him toward the corner near the window. "And you—over there," I pointed to my daughter, "what seems to be the major issue here?"

"Aubrey hit me," Aidan claimed, his dark brows furrowed and jaw ticking.

"I did not!" my daughter screamed back, her fists firmly planted on her hips. You gotta love it when your kids look like perfect miniatures of you, and Aubrey certainly does. Right down to the indignant fist-on-hips pose.

"Are you two really fighting about fried potatoes?" I questioned, my eyes darting back and forth between the two of them.

Sheepish smirks crept across their faces. "Yeah, sounds

pretty stupid when I put it like that, doesn't it?" Aubrey shot a daggery look across the room at her brother. In turn, he stuck his tongue out at her. *Ah, yes, sibling rivalry at its finest.*

"Tell him to stop sticking out his tongue at me!" my daughter screeched at an eardrum-bursting level.

"Look, I am having a Mommy Day over here, trying to read my book, and you two are ruining it. I don't care who is Team French Fry and who is Team Tater Tot, and I don't care who started it. I am ending it RIGHT NOW. Both of you go to your rooms, and I don't want to hear a freaking word from either one of you till dinner, where we will not be indulging in either of the aforementioned potato products. You'll be lucky if you get more than bread and water to drink!"

Aidan shook his head while Aubrey began crafting some crocodile tears. I could see them shining in the corners of her eyes as she prepared to wail about how unfair I was being. "Nope, not one more word. Go!" I yelled at them. Their chins lowered, eyes downcast, the two made their way down the hall to the staircase in an orderly single file.

"Damn kids," I muttered under my breath after they left the room. I was about to blame David for knocking me up, but then I remembered I begged him for kids. He hadn't really been on board with the whole offspring thing, but I had reminded him how cool it would be to have mini versions of us roaming around with our DNA they could pass on to future minions of their own. *Yeah, real cool*, I chuckled as I made myself comfortable again in my reading chair.

Being married to an architect has its perks. Since we

moved into 6 Juniper Court, we've made quite a few improvements to our house. David built me the most amazing reading nook. It seriously looks like something from a Pinterest board with its floor-to-ceiling mahogany bookcases; thick, luxurious velvet drapes, and literally the most comfortable chaise lounge I have ever had the pleasure of lying on. There's a small desk where I pay our bills and write both titillating and scathing book and product reviews (depending on which is warranted, of course).

I also pen a blog from that desk: Valley Archer Design. In some ways it's an anti-mommy blog because it features high-end shit that most kids would probably destroy. Now that my kids are older, I can actually have nice stuff again, so that is pretty awesome if I do say so myself.

So where was I? I asked myself as I scanned the open page on my Kindle. *Oh, yes.* The heroine just made some coy, but not particularly subtle remark about how she wouldn't mind getting to know the hero better. It's implied that she meant without clothes. *Well, duh.*

My eyes grew wide as the hero proceeded to ask the heroine what she would think about his business associate joining in on the action. *What will she say? Will she be into it?* I wondered as my gaze quickly danced across the lines of text at a record pace.

Oh, my god, she's into it! I cheered as the heroine led the two men down the hallway to her bedroom. She lit two candles and told the men to make themselves comfortable. I felt a tingle traipse down my spine and straight into my core as my thighs clenched together. I couldn't wait to see what happened next.

I repositioned, spreading the Kindle on my lap, and my hand absentmindedly wandered into the space between my hips, which was beginning to burn with desire as the scene in her bedroom unfolded before my eyes. Clothes began to fly off. Certain male appendages came gloriously springing forth from unbuttoned trousers. Bosoms heaved. Soft gasps filled the air.

Holy fuck, this is hot, I thought as I continued to devour each and every succulent word. I was finally getting to the point where the heroine spread herself on her back, imploring the two dashing, well-muscled men to have their way with her when I heard the garage door squeak open.

Oh no! I tossed my Kindle onto the chaise as I scrambled to my feet. David was home. Early, no less. And I hadn't even started dinner yet. *Shit!*

It wasn't until much later that evening, after the dishes were done, the kitchen cleaned, and the children tucked into bed, that I was able to pull out my Kindle and resume the steamy *ménage a trois* scene I'd been enjoying earlier. I was totally engrossed in admiring the heroine's adept handling of two massive cocks when David slipped into bed and turned off the light. He stroked his warm hand down my thigh as I continued reading, my eyes bulging at the lengths this tenacious character would go to please both of her men.

"Sex scene?" David asked, trailing his fingers back up my thighs until they landed right next door to my pussy. All I'd have to do is shift my hips a bit, and his hand would probably slip down to where an ache was building in my core, the same one that started to smoke during my earlier reading session.

"Valley?" he questioned again when I failed to answer him.

"Mmmhmmm," I finally replied, the smooth consonants vibrating between my lips.

"Really sexy?" he verified. David was well aware of my reading habits and sometimes even enjoyed it when I read passages aloud to him in bed. Many a satisfying romp had begun with reading a scene from one of my favorite books and ended with acting it out between the sheets.

He contested my silence by leaning over to press his lips against my neck. Then he followed up that maneuver with kisses down my collarbone and chest, planting them one by one until his mouth landed on my full, heaving breasts. My squeal pierced the still, quiet air when his teeth sank into my nipple, sending a wave of desire gushing down to my pussy.

"Is she getting some cock?" he growled against my enflamed flesh as I waited for his teeth to grip my nipple between them again.

"Oh yes," I gasped as the shock came and dissipated again, like a candle being snuffed out. But the thrill remained and reverberated through me, just like a bit of smoke trails away when a flame is extinguished. "She's getting two cocks, actually."

"Mmm...two cocks are better than one," David pointed out, his hot breath teasing my nipple into an almost uncontrollable frenzy.

"I would think so." Anything else I wanted to say was trapped in my throat when his teeth sank into the tender flesh of my nipple yet again. Now my sex was completely flooded with desire, longing for contact as I pulled his body on top of me.

David is tall with a lean, runner's body and muscles in all the right places. I loved the way my ample size sixteen curves sank into his firm, sculpted chest and strong limbs. I felt at home as he wrapped his arms around me, holding me close to him as he kissed my neck again and the swell of his cock pressed against my thigh.

"Please, baby," was all I could manage to get out as I writhed beneath him, waiting to be filled.

"Those books really get you going, don't they?" He stroked a finger down my cheek. He loves making me wait for it.

I moaned out a yes against the stubble that had grown since he shaved that morning. The way it scraped against my chin sent another shiver of desire coursing through me. *Why did he have to be so damn sexy with his gorgeous, plump lips and piercing hazel eyes?*

I stroked my fingers through his thick, dark hair, which was just starting to show a few strands of silver as he approached his 37th birthday. I planned on dyeing mine for eternity. I would never succumb to gray hair, but on David it looked so damn sexy highlighting his temples and widow's peak.

He was a fucking gorgeous man, and I was one lucky woman. I wrapped my legs around him, urging him with my persistent moans. "Don't you want me?"

"Do you wish you had another cock here? One to wrap your lips around while I plunge mine deep inside you?" he asked in a raspy voice.

The mental image his question inspired lit up like a marquis in my mind. I could envision another man beside me, on his knees, thrusting his rock-hard cock out for me to lick while David fucked me. The idea of two men taking pleasure from my body at the same time nearly took me over the edge, and David wasn't even inside me yet.

"Oh, yes...baby...yes, I wanna try two cocks," I answered, my hips bucking against him as I silently begged for him to take me.

"I think I'd like to watch that," he answered, and I swear his cock throbbed even more insistently against me as the vision filled his mind. In one swift motion, he impaled me, his granite-hard tool finding passage inside me as he pushed to the very depths, causing me to cry out.

"Shhhh, the kids..." he whispered as he stilled inside me.

"Damn it, fuck me!" I sighed, the words coming out in a hoarse whisper.

"As you wish." He obliged, moving again with shallow strokes.

"Fuck me harder, baby!" I bucked against him again, gripping his hips to push him deeper and faster.

"Maybe you do need two cocks to satisfy you, my little nympho." He chuckled as he withdrew and pulled me to the side of the bed. He lifted my hips and dragged me to the very edge before plunging back inside of me. Using my hips for leverage, he pounded me senseless, delivering more and more power with every stroke as he chased his release.

I lost track of how many orgasms I had as I imagined having him and another man tag-team me. In my fantasy the other man was the contractor David usually worked with—a handsome silver fox and all around fine specimen. I envisioned him stroking his cock and waiting for his turn at me as David drilled into me, deeper, harder, faster…

LUNCHES PACKED, BREAKFAST MADE, I LOOKED AROUND THE kitchen with a sense of accomplishment. Mornings were approximately one thousand percent better if I had gotten laid the night before. Add that to a piping hot cup of—not coffee, of course—tea, and I was truly an unstoppable force.

I swear, if my kids knew what sex was, they'd always recognize the morning after I got some, because I am unbearably perky. I can imagine the eyerolls I'm going to get when they become teenagers. At that point, they probably will put two and two together. They're pretty bright kids, after all.

I heard David rushing down the steps before I actually saw him. I glanced over to make sure his eggs and bacon were still on the counter, ready to serve him as soon as he sat down at our cozy kitchen table. We hardly ever ate in our beautiful mahogany-trimmed dining room; it was much too formal.

I was beyond pleased with the renovations we'd done in the kitchen. It was airy, bright, and modern, with natural sunlight streaming through the glass French doors that led to the back deck. There was another entrance to the deck off the adjacent living room and to the patio below it from our walk-out basement. The outdoor spaces at our house were perfect for entertaining.

Our kitchen had been upgraded with stainless steel

appliances and a stunning black granite countertop, the only dark fixture in the entire space. It was sleek and shiny like my Mustang and my hair, and gleamed like a mirror when it was nice and polished. We'd also had the cabinets painted a rich, creamy ivory and added a tiled backsplash with a lovely mosaic design that incorporated my accent colors of apple green and marine blue. Finally, David had hung a pot rack over the island, which freed up an incredible amount of space in the lower cabinets. Now if I could just train the kids to put everything in its rightful place when they unloaded the dishwasher, it would truly be my dream kitchen.

Sometimes I didn't mind this whole 50s housewife scenario. You know, having breakfast and dinner on the table at precise times and packing everyone's lunches in the morning, each one with a Hershey's kiss to remind them they were missed at home while they toiled through their busy work/school days. I didn't mind schlepping the laundry up and down the stairs or scrubbing the kitchen till it sparkled.

It's just that I felt something was lacking. My blog filled a bit of my time, as did my smutty romance novels, but it still seemed like something was missing. I wasn't expecting motherhood and marriage to be a whirlwind adventure, but I did miss the anticipation of a big night out or a last minute get away.

David leaned in to press a kiss on my cheek before taking a seat at the table. I smiled as I set his gold-rimmed plate down in front of him and was pleased to see the steam still rising off the meat and eggs. The kids had already eaten and were upstairs brushing their teeth and gathering up their school supplies to stuff into their backpacks before loading up in the Mustang for our morning trek to school.

"Did you mean what you said last night?" I asked, disturbing David's intent study of something on his phone.

"What do you mean, sweetheart?" He glanced up, pinning his gaze to mine.

I couldn't deny I'd been thinking about it all morning. Still fantasizing about David's contractor...which was a tiny detail I would never mention to David, but... damn. I had already predicted he had a yummy six-pack, and, of course, he just had to be well-hung.

"Uh, the threesome?" I raised my brows as the thundering footsteps of my offspring bounded down the stairs. *Oh, god,* my body flooded with panic. I really hoped they hadn't heard what I said.

My husband's nose scrunched and lips pursed. "That was just..." He mouthed the words "dirty talk" as Aidan slipped into the kitchen to grab his lunch off the counter.

"But..." was all that came out of my mouth as Aubrey stalked behind me, then threw her arms around my waist, squeezing me so tightly I thought I might lose my breakfast all over the table.

David's lips quirked at his daughter, who released me from her talon-like grip and then swooped over to her father for an equally vise-like embrace. "Hope you have a good day, Daddy!" she cooed, planting a kiss on his cheek.

"You too, honey," he echoed back.

Once the kids went to the foyer to put on their shoes, I returned my gaze to David. "But wouldn't it be exciting?"

"Do I get a threesome too?" he asked, whispering the appropriate word.

"I guess so…" I hadn't really thought about what it would be like with another woman in our bed, but what's good for the goose is good for the gander. *Right?*

"Okay, set it up," he said as if we were making a business deal. He placed his fork on his plate and rose to carry his dirty dishes to the sink.

I stood there in disbelief. *Did my husband actually just give me permission to find us a third?*

I'm what some people call a Type A personality. What that really means is I don't pussy-foot around. When I want to do something, I get the fucking wheels in motion by any means necessary. I guess you could say I take the bull by the horn, and that's whether I'm hosting a dinner party, organizing a bake sale, or trying to figure out how to arrange a threesome.

At first I didn't put two and two together. I kept thinking what I wanted was a *ménage a trois*, but then I remembered what David said about another girl. I'd be kind of an asshole if I made this all about me. And trust me, I do that sometimes and David always indulges me, because that's what a ridiculously awesome husband he is. But most of the time I try to give as good as I get. He was open-minded enough to give me the green light, so the least I could do was try to make sure he had something in the mix to look forward to, right?

So, swinging. That's what I was really talking about, right? *How do you become a swinger?*

I sort of assumed right away there was no official workshop or class you could take. *Swinging 101,* I laughed just thinking of it. Though I wouldn't be surprised if some sort of initiation rites or good-natured hazing were involved. Was there a guild? A fraternity we could join? Where did these people hang out? Where could you find them in the wild?

While waiting to pick the kids up from school, I grabbed my trusty phone out of my purse and began to do a couple of Google searches: *How do you become a swinger? How do you meet swingers?*

Please stop for a moment to appreciate the full hilarity of me perusing educational sites on swinging while waiting to pick my children up from school. Remember the book *Everything I Needed to Know, I Learned in Kinder-garten?* I'm sure learning to share with others was right up there on that dude's list.

So Google led me pretty swiftly to an article called "7 Steps to Swinging."

1. Figure out why you want to swing.

Uh...because I want to fuck other guys? And I think I'd like to watch David nail some other chick. That would be hot. Should there be other reasons than this? 'Cause I can't really think of any.

2. Figure out how you want to swing.

I'm thinking by the dude putting his penis in my vagina. That way. Oh, wait, it really means WHERE you want to swing —like parties or cruises or just meeting couples for dinner. Hmm. I like parties. Cruises are good. Dinners are awesome too. See? I'm open-minded as fuck. I'm already a boss at this.

. . .

3. SET SOME GROUND RULES.

I'm good with please *and* thank you. *Oh, it means between you and your partner. Okay, yeah, that is something David and I will have to discuss, but, in general, he just goes along with whatever I want. I married the perfect man!*

4. WORK ON BUILDING UP YOUR CONFIDENCE.

Welp, I'm not lacking in that department. Might have to work on David a bit.

5. CONSIDER MEETING PEOPLE ONLINE FIRST.

You can do this online? WHAT? Well, who the fuck would have thought of that? There are apparently websites dedicated to swinging. Sign me up, baby! Sign me up!

I DON'T GET PAST NUMBER FIVE BECAUSE AUBREY BEGAN pounding on my window, asking me to unlock the doors. *Oops.* That was pretty much a #momfail. I unlocked the doors to my Stang, and the kids piled in from opposite sides, dumping their stuff in the middle of the back seat so as to form a veritable wall between each other. *The sibling love is strong between these two. /sarcasm*

"How was your day, kids?" I asked in my perkiest, sing-songy voice. They were going to think I've nailed this mom thing when they got home and saw I'd made them homemade cookies that afternoon!

"Fine," Aidan mumbled, then turned his head to stare out the window.

"Social studies sucks," Aubrey complained, then she turned and did the same as her brother. If I wanted to start World War III, I would have just mentioned she was copying him, and it would be on like Donkey Kong.

Well, so much for facilitating a sparkling after-school conversation. Hopefully milk and cookies would cheer everyone up, even if it did ruin their dinner.

DAVID HAD A BOARD MEETING THAT NIGHT FOR ONE OF THE charity groups he was involved in. He promised me when we moved to Sunview he wasn't going to go crazy overextending himself like he had in our previous town. But on our very first day here, literally the day we moved in, he was asked by two different neighbors to get involved in two different organizations. Evidently he has SUCKER written all over his face!

I remember one of the wives turning to me to ask if I wanted to get involved in some lame save the fruit bats campaign or something equally ridiculous, but it was pretty clear from the look on my face what my thoughts were on the matter.

Some people have issues saying no. I am not one of those people. No wonder I want to try swinging; I want to be able to say yes for a change. *Yes, yes, yes!*

I managed to quiet the kids down and put them to task doing homework, mostly because I bribed them with an episode of some TV show David disapproves of as a reward. I tiptoed into David's office so as not to attract any undesired attention. I swear every time I do anything, Aubrey thinks she needs to be right there shadowing me. I love that girl to pieces, but damn, I just want to take a breath of my own air every once in a while!

I remember the day I finally got to use the bathroom without a child watching me. It was a glorious, glorious day, and I recall thinking, *This is it. I'm going to survive motherhood after all.* It was touch and go there for a few years between the lack of privacy and wiping dirty bums.

I settled myself into the soft leather executive chair in my husband's office and opened his laptop. I couldn't remember the swinging sites recommended in the article I was reading earlier, so as usual, I put my faith in Google to show me the way. I typed in *meet swingers online* and holy hell, you should see some of the shit that popped up on my screen! Apparently there are NO parental controls on David's laptop – *duly noted*!

I clicked on one that looked interesting. It touted its ability to "Find Swingers in Sunview!" so I felt like I was on the right track. On the homepage it asked me to confirm I was 18 years of age, so I did. Then it took me to another page that questioned whether or not I was a mature, professional, discreet individual who wanted to explore my wildest fantasies.

Yes, yes, yes! I thought again as I clicked the button to learn more.

First I had to make a profile. The last profile I made was for Pinterest, which by the way, I hate almost as much as yoga and Starbucks, but my ridiculous yuppie but hipster-wanna-be little sister made me get on there to look at her wedding board. *Blech.* How can someone be both a yuppie and a hipster at the same time? She's a *Yupster*.

So back to the profile. The first box asked for username.

Oh, shit. Everyone knows coming up with the user-name is the absolute hardest part of online profile creation. I was so skipping that until the very end. The next section asked me to check a box for male, female or couple. *Couple.* Whew, I totally had this. Then I had to enter David's details. Height: 6'1". *I like my men tall, dark and handsome!* Hair: Brown. Eyes: Hazel. Build: Muscular/Athletic. *Oh, yeah, baby, my man is HOT!* Age: 36. Orientation: Straight

Okay, my details were next. Height: 5'8". *Mama's got some height on her too!* Hair: Black. Eyes: Green. Build: Curvy. *Hell, yeah! Curves are where it's at!* Age: 34. Orientation: Straight. *Hmm. Bi-curious? Uh. Well, maybe.* I clicked that instead. I hated to rule anything out this early in the game.

I scanned the next section, which asked for a summary of what we were interested in. Extemporaneously, I came up with, "Attractive professional couple in our mid-30's seeks other open-minded couples for fun and sexy times. We'll show you ours if you show us yours! Let's get to know each other."

That sounds okay, right? I could always go back and edit it later. Then it asked for a photo. Well, I couldn't exactly upload a photo of our faces. I mean, this was supposed to be on the *downlow*, right? I should have checked to see what kinds of photos other couples have posted, but it wouldn't let me view other profiles until ours was created. Would it let me leave it blank?

I hit submit, and the username box started flashing red. *Oh, yeah,* I remembered, hoping a brainstorm would produce something brilliant. *Hey, it's been known to happen.*

So… David is an architect, and when we moved to Sunview about nine months ago, he promised it was going to be just like paradise. I wasn't quite in agreement with him on the paradise part. I mean, so far all I'd seen of Sunview were nosy neighbors, snobby soccer moms, and a freaking Starbucks on every corner. But if Sunview did indeed have a dark and naughty side…a sexy, sinful side… then maybe, just maybe, it could be paradise.

Every time I get a bee in my bonnet, David always says I have a new project. He'd probably say that about this too, that swinging is my new project.

I took a deep breath as my fingers hovered over the keys. *ProjectParadise,* I typed in the box. *That's our username.*

BY THE TIME DAVID GOT HOME FROM HIS BOARD MEETING, the kids had already been tucked into bed. I hoped he'd pass on giving them a goodnight kiss so he wouldn't wake them up, but one look at his sad little face made me change my mind. How could I resist the eyes of a man who just wanted to kiss his babies goodnight?

"Aidan told me you let them watch that show again. You don't think they're a little too young for it?" he asked, returning to the living room where I was curled up with my Kindle, getting ready to start another book. I figured that was the only way to get over the book hangover I was suffering from the one I just finished.

"Oh, David, don't be so overprotective! They'll be fine. I already told them it's not real. It's a cartoon for fuck's sake!"

"The problem is it might be a little too real, even if it's supposed to be funny. I hate to think they understand any of it, but they probably do. I hate the idea of their innocence being destroyed."

"You didn't mind destroying my innocence," I teased him, giving him a devilish smirk.

He laughed so hard, I thought he might wake the kids up. "Hardly! If anything, it's *you* who corrupted *me*!"

David and I met in college where we were both students in the most impossible statistics class ever. He tutored me, otherwise I would have almost certainly failed. By the end of the semester, I was calculating the probability we would be shopping for engagement rings over the summer. It was high, very high.

We were one of those couples who focused on our careers before having kids. We got married fresh out of college, but spent the next five years socking away money and enjoying coupledom. I was pretty settled with David, loving our lives together. And I loved my career as an interior designer. The only thing I didn't like was the constant question of "When are you two going to settle down and have kids?"

First off, having two professional careers, a mortgage and two car payments sounds pretty damn settled to me already, but for some reason people think you're not a real family unless you pop a couple kids out of your vagina. As soon as you squeeze out one little rug rat, they're asking you when you're going to make him a sister. And after creating two tiny humans, people start asking, "You're not going to have any MORE, are you?" Apparently having two is the requisite number. Gotta love it when your family and friends have a better idea of what I should be doing with my vagina and breasts at various stages of my life than I do.

Maybe that's why I want to take charge of them so badly now. After so many years of using ovulation predictors, being forced to fuck on certain dates, then having a tiny, ravenous mouth gumming at my nipples for months on end, I can finally say all those body parts are mine. I can finally do with them as I please.

And what I please to do is have more sex. I haven't been able to get my fill for the past couple years now. Poor David—I know he affectionately calls me his Little Nympho, but sometimes I detect the slightest twinge of resentment behind it. "Again tonight, honey?" he sometimes complains when I stroke my hands down his chest all the way to his cock. Imagine my disappointment when that bastard doesn't want to come out and play. He'll just hang out, all sheepishly tucked inside, not wanting anything to do with me. It's not exactly good for the old self-esteem.

I know it's not me, though. I'm a reasonably attractive woman. Okay, screw that. I'm a pretty hot MILF—if you happen to like big tits, a curvy ass, and thick thighs. And I know a lot of men go for that, because I find their eyes on me every time we go out. Hell, our neighbor Sully checks out my ass every time I walk across the street to get the mail. His wife Nina would shit a brick if she ever saw him ogling me like he does.

"Valley?" My thoughts dissipated as David crossed the

room toward me. "Sorry I was so late getting home tonight. I didn't realize our meeting would run so long."

Some women might be a little...concerned...if their husbands regularly stayed late at work or had to go to various "committee" meetings a night or two a week. They might think he was having an affair or something. First off, I've seen David's secretary, a thoroughly competent bespectacled lady in her early 60s, as well as his female associate, who happens to be a rather masculine-looking lesbian. The only other people he spends a lot of time with are his general contractor (the silver fox in my fantasy) and his clients. Unless there was someone else in his building he was screwing around with, I'm pretty sure his excuses are legit.

"It's okay, babe," I told him, uncrossing my legs and re-crossing them, à la Sharon Stone in *Basic Instinct*. I was wearing a short denim skirt and a little fitted t-shirt. And hell no, there were no panties underneath. I lost those and my bra right after I put the kids in bed.

My nipples were standing at attention, insistently pressed against the thin fabric of my t-shirt. I could tell he was trying not to stare, but his eyes were zeroing in anyway, like my areolas had bullseyes painted on them.

"The good news is Bill thinks he can convince the board to hire me to design their new building," he told me. His eyes were gleaming, but not from his perusal of my nipples, unfortunately. He was caught up in the excitement of his work news.

"Oh, that's great," I answered, putting my Kindle down beside me. Once David decides he's ready to tell me about his day, he can go on a while. I was 99% certain reading time was done for the night. "Wait, what building?"

"Bill O'Hair," David reminded me. "You know, the priest?"

"Priest?"

He laughed and nodded as he took a seat on the sofa cushion next to me. "Yes, honey, you know, the guys who wear black with the white collars and absolve people of their sins? They hang out in confessionals."

"So you mean like a church? You're going to design a church?" I confirmed.

He nodded again, still smiling so wide his hazel eyes nearly crinkled shut. "Their old building downtown has fallen into disrepair, and while it's got beautiful classic architecture, their congregation has grown so much in the past few years, they figure it's better to start from scratch. They recently secured about twenty acres on the outskirts of town and are now looking for someone to draw up the plans. That's where I come in!"

"I'm sure you do," I winked at him. *I can turn just about anything into sexual innuendo. It's a gift.*

"I am supposed to make it look traditional, yet modern." He chuckled. "I love it when they ask for the impossible. It's like a bald guy going to the barber and asking to come away looking like Justin Bieber."

"Oh, honey, if anyone can do it, it's you," I cooed, climbing onto his lap so I straddled him with a knee on each side of his thighs. This is a pretty incredible position for sex, but with all the lights on and this close to bedtime, I'm too afraid we'll hear the little pitter-patter of feet coming down to get a drink of water if we decide to do it now.

"So what did you do today?" he asked. "Besides baking cookies and corrupting our kids with television?"

"You better watch it, buddy, or no cookies for you!" I said, doing my best Soup Nazi impression from *Seinfeld*.

"Oh, there's some left?" His eyes lit up just like Aidan's did when I revealed my cookie stash earlier. *Like father, like son*, I mused.

"Yes, but you can't have one until I show you something!" I jumped off his lap and tugged at his hand until he rose, then I dragged him into his office where the laptop was still open to the screen where I'd created our swinger profile. *Oops*, I realized as soon as I saw it. I should have probably closed that sucker.

"What's this?"

I pulled out his leather chair and gestured for him to sit. "Take a look at this, honey. See what you think."

I watched his eyes dart over the words. "What does this mean?" he asked, pointing to the flashing letter graphic in the corner of the screen.

"Oh, we have mail!" I gasp. I hadn't had a chance to check back since I'd gotten busy with the kids.

He clicked on the icon, and an inbox opened where there was a message from a couple named "sunviewswingers." *Well, that's a real creative username*, I scoffed under my breath.

"Hey there," David read out loud, "welcome to the site. We see you're in Sunview as well. We'd love to grab a drink sometime!"

I raised my eyebrows and waited for David to turn and lock gazes with me. He shrugged, then directed his eyes back to the screen. "Click on their profile," I suggested as he continued to poke around the site.

He clicked on their username, which loaded their profile. There was a photo of tits. Very tan tits with pointy brown nipples. "Wait, that's it?" I asked, confused. How were we supposed to know if we wanted to fuck these people if there were no photos? *Ahem.* Real photos? Like of body parts *I* might be interested in?

"Can we write them back and ask for photos?" he questioned.

I shrugged. "I guess so. I don't really know the protocol here. I'm kinda new at this." I laughed and wrapped my arms around his neck, then leaned down over his shoulder as he returned to the message in our inbox.

"Thanks for your message. Do you have any other photos you could share?" he said aloud as he typed. He signed it *D & V* because they had signed their message *E & S*. *We're quick learners, obvs.*

Not more than thirty seconds later, we heard a ding, and the mail icon flashed again. His eyes sparkled with excitement as he clicked to open the message.

This time I read, "Well, you don't have ANY photos, but we see you're new. Just in general though, it's not polite to ask for more photos when you don't have any at all. We unlocked our private photos for you. Please upload some and unlock yours for us as well. Thanks, E & S."

"Private photos?" I quirked a brow. "That sounds... interesting. How do we get to those?"

David navigated back to their profile and saw a little icon that looked like a photo album, which we surmised were the private photos. Sure enough, when he clicked on it, several thumbnails appeared. E and S were an attractive, very tan couple in their mid-fifties. He had a silver goatee and bald head, and she had dyed auburn hair that fell in wispy layers framing her face. They also seemed quite comfortable in their own skin, judging by all the nude photos of them.

"Well, what do you think?" David questioned, looking up at me.

"They seem a little old for us, but otherwise okay. What do you think?" I answered.

"Maybe older is better. You know, to show us the ropes. They seem like they've been doing this for a while."

I rubbed my hands together. "Good point. Okay, so what's next?"

"I guess we write back and set a date for...drinks? Dinner?"

"Sounds like a plan! Let's do this!"

$\mathcal{H}$ 3 $\mathcal{H}$

What does one wear on their first swinger date? I asked myself as I fumbled through my closet looking for appropriate swinger attire. When we uploaded our first photos to the site, we learned pretty quickly that "anything goes" as far as nudity on the site was concerned.

We took a pretty classy naked selfie of just our chests. We threw that up as our profile photo, then we had a blast doing a little photo shoot to fill out our private photo album with some sexy shots. I dressed up in some lingerie and David in some silk boxers and we just went to town. It's a good thing our kids didn't wake up during our photo shoot, because I'm not sure how we would have explained it.

I was pretty sure the nudity standard set by the swinging website would not be welcomed at the restaurant where we were meeting E & S, whose real names were Ed and Shawna, FYI. I settled on a short black skirt and an off-the-shoulder zebra print top with strappy black heels. It was getting too warm to wear my favorite black knee-high boots. *A damn shame.* I guessed I'd have to put them away until next fall. I went to apply my makeup as David came out of the shower with nothing but a towel wrapped around his waist.

He looked so sexy standing there with tiny glistening water droplets clinging to his perfectly toned muscles that I almost wanted to stay there and lick all the water off him instead of going out. His eyes met mine, and he gave me a look that seemed to say, "Really?"

I nodded, though he hadn't actually said a word.

He chuckled under his breath as he moved to his dresser and began to pull a pair of boxers and socks from his top drawer. He liked to tease me by putting on the boxers underneath his towel so I couldn't sneak a peek at his package. Then he glanced back at me with a deliciously mischievous smirk on his face.

A man's routine for getting ready for a night out is nothing like a woman's. They literally shower and put on clothes. Any clothes. Like no one cares what they are wearing. How often do you go out on the town and think, *whoa, that dude is really wearing the hell out of those pants?* No, but you might think he has a nice ass. Or at least I do. That is a pretty regular thought I have, actually.

David grabbed a pair of khaki pants from his closet and then turned around to slide them on, so I once again could not see the goods. *Oh, he thinks he's so clever and coy.* I shook my head in pretend exasperation as he pulled a black button-down shirt from the closet and slid it over his undershirt. He buttoned it and rolled up his sleeves, then presented me with a gleaming smile. "I'm ready!"

I was, of course, still scurrying around trying to find shoes and jewelry and figure out what was going on with my hair. I usually straighten it, but decided to leave it wavy for a change. I liked the way it rustled around my shoulders while I dug through my jewelry box for a silver necklace and matching earrings. While I was in deep debate about the silver filigree or the onyx with silver accents, David grabbed me from behind and wheeled me around to face him.

"Whatever happens tonight," he said, taking my hands into his and looking deep into my eyes, "I want you to know I love you. And nothing will ever change that."

Awwwww. I was sure my heart just melted into a pile of goo all over the floor. "I love you too, darling," I returned the sentiment. I stretched up to plant a kiss on his cheek.

"You can do better than that," he said, the corners of his lips turning up.

"Is that so?"

He pulled me into his arms and pressed his hot, moist lips against mine, urging my mouth open with his tongue. It was the kind of kiss that leaves you breathless. I was so hot and bothered by the time he pulled away, I nearly forgot where we were, what we were doing, or who the hell I even was.

I knew one thing: no matter what this couple was like, there was no way "E" was as good of a kisser as "D."

I NEVER THOUGHT I'D BE SITTING IN THE LOBBY OF A restaurant with my husband, waiting to meet a couple we were considering fucking. I know we all have bucket lists, but the items on them are often these vague, sparkly, abstract notions. They usually aren't the type of things where you make a step-by-step plan and then work your way through each step.

For us, it was Step 1: Make an account on a swinger site. Step 2: Wait for a potentially matching couple to contact us. Step 3: Meet them at a restaurant to discuss said fucking. It all seems so logical, so linear.

I always thought these things happened at some wild, drunken party that turns into an orgy, where you don't consciously consider all of the consequences before jumping in head first. *Or would that be vag first?*

"I think that's them," David said, leaning down to whisper into my ear. A smile spread across my face as I glanced up at the crowd, trying to locate two needles in the haystack with Ed and Shawna's faces.

Bingo, I spotted an older couple making their way around the bar toward us. He was a little shorter than I envisioned, and she was a bit rounder. They both had captivating smiles, though, their eyes crinkling as they zeroed in on us sitting on the leather-covered benches in the restaurant's lobby.

I jumped up, David right behind me, and extended my hand. Ed swooped down on me, throwing his arms around me and pulling me in for a big bear hug, punctuated by a kiss on each cheek. David's brows furrowed a bit as he gave Shawna a pat on the back and a timid kiss hello on the cheek, except she turned at the last second so that their lips brushed together awkwardly. I wanted to burst out laughing, but managed to bury the sound deep in my throat.

"Did you put your name in for a table yet?" Shawna inquired, and David nodded his head. I could see he was eager to erase her memory of the failed smooch hello.

Ed stood so close to me while David approached the hostess stand to let them know our party had arrived, that I had to seriously question whether or not he understood the concept of personal space. Shawna just beamed at my husband's ass as if she was already making a list of things she planned to do to him later.

When the hostess collected four menus, I jumped ahead to slide my hand under David's elbow, so he could properly escort me to our table. Ed and Shawna followed behind, and I forced myself to refrain from glancing back to see the expressions on their faces. Once the four of us settled in the booth, David and I across the table from Ed and Shawna, I felt like we could "officially" start. The greeting had been a bit weird and ill-timed, but this was the real introduction, the real test.

There were a few pleasantries: Ed and Shawna told us their children were in college, and that they were originally from Michigan. We shared that our children were in elementary school, and they made wistful eyes at how quickly children grow up. Then our waitress stopped by to take our drink order, and it felt like it was time to get down to brass tacks.

"How long have you guys been on the site?" Ed asked, his fingers interlaced on top of the table. Shawna's hands were not visible, and I had a feeling why: she was stroking up and down Ed's legs and who knows where else under the table.

"We just joined the first night you sent us a message," I

explained. "We're like virgins at this swinging thing!" I whispered the S word, of course. No one was going to accuse me of being indiscreet.

"Wow, we love taking couples' virginities!" Shawna cooed, looking at Ed with lusty eyes.

"Oh, yes, we consider it our specialty, in fact," Ed beamed, glancing back down at her with an equal amount of passion.

"So how long have you guys been doing this…and how did you get involved?" David asked, reaching beneath the tabletop to take my hand into his. I felt my body flood with his warmth as he laced his fingers through mine.

Ed deferred to his wife, whose face lit up with a devious smile. "I think it's been…what, honey? At least ten years now. We started up back in the olden days, before the internet made it so easy. You could just go to a club every weekend and see who was around to get into trouble with. Now there's all these sites and Facebook groups and meet and greets and cruises to go on. People talk online and make plans to meet, text and sext until the cows come home. I think it takes a bit of the spontaneity and excitement out of it, but on the other hand, I guess you can't be too careful in this day and age."

My eyebrows immediately quirked. "What do you mean?"

She pursed her lips and turned to Ed. I loved how they communicated with each other so well without even saying a word. Only couples who were really in tune had those kinds of skills. "Whenever you get a group of people together, there's always going to be an odd one in the bunch. Usually they're harmless, but we've seen some real drama in some of the groups we've tried out. Some are really cliquish; some have a lot of creepy single guys; still others –"

Shawna cut him off. "Some single lady we know got catfished by this supposed lifestyle guy in some foreign country. Was it Romania, honey?"

"Hungary, I think. Maybe Czech Republic... Anyway... the lifestyle isn't for the faint of heart, but we enjoy it. We wouldn't have it any other way."

"Lifestyle? Is that what you guys call it?" David asked.

"Yeah, it's a little more discreet than swinging...and not as, you know, loaded. Swinging just sounds like 70s-era key parties to me. And we abbreviate it LS a lot, too, especially on social media and in texts and that sort of thing."

I felt like we were interviewing them more than anything else. If I were a journalist, I could write a pretty shocking exposé using this info. Guess it's a good thing I'm not...but then again, I could see why you had to be careful. I suddenly wondered if we needed to worry about people at David's work finding out. Or our neighbors... *Oh god, the neighbors.*

"So you didn't say how you got into it originally?" My eyes darted between Ed's pale green ones and Shawna's sparkling baby blues.

"Oh, gosh, it's been so long now," Shawna answered, and wide grins spread across both of their faces. "We had some neighbors a long time ago back in this little development where we used to live in East Lansing. They were into it and invited us to a party, and the rest was history."

"So what about you guys?" Ed asked. "Why do you

want to get involved? Do you guys have naughty neighbors too?"

David turned toward me, his lips curling up as I chuckled. "Oh, god no, not that we know of. At least not yet. I guess I'm trying to figure out if we will be ostracized from the neighborhood if anyone finds out."

"Let me give you a piece of advice our neighbors gave us back in the day," Ed offered. "To hell with everyone else. You guys do what makes YOU happy!"

"I love that advice!" I beamed, noticing my cheeks were already sore from smiling. I really did like these two, even if I was having trouble envisioning either of them naked. They seemed genuine, caring, and a lot of fun. I wondered if we could just skip ahead to a lifelong friendship where they unlocked the doors to the secret swinger...ahem...lifestyle club, and let us in.

Two hours later, we had barely touched our food, but we had managed to each drink three or four cocktails apiece, which were no doubt going to my head. I wasn't quite to the point of slurring words, but I was well past the *everything is freaking hilarious* stage. That was when Ed and Shawna started sharing their rules with us.

"We're full swap, same room most of the time until we really get to know you. Condoms are a must; kissing is okay; oral is good – no anal. Ed here likes to dabble in some light BDSM while I'm totally bi, and I especially love squirters," Shawna explained, her blue eyes flashing.

"Whoa, can we get a translation on that?" David asked, taking a sip of his water. He and Ed had stopped drinking alcohol during the last round so they'd be able to drive our drunk asses home at some point.

Ed grinned. "Full swap means we go all the way with a couple. Some folks are soft swap, which means they do everything except vaginal sex. We do full, as long as the guys wear condoms. We don't mind kissing with other couple, especially the two girls. Some couples will let the girls kiss, but not the opposite non-married couples."

"What?!" My eyebrows immediately flew up. "No kissing? Why?"

"Some couples feel like it's too intimate," Shawna explained, rolling her eyes. Her opinion on the practice was pretty obvious.

"More intimate than putting your mouth on someone else's genitals or putting your dick in their pussy?" I questioned, pursing my lips. I was having trouble understanding this.

Shawna shrugged. "Some couples like to keep some things special and just for the two of them, like vaginal intercourse or kissing. For us it's anal. I only do that with Ed." She leaned closer to me with her hand on one side of her mouth so Ed wouldn't be able to read her lips. "And he's not hung like a horse down there, so I can handle him with no problem. Some of these lifestyle dudes…I swear… they're carrying baseball bats down there! Imagine that in your chocolate starfish!"

I almost spit out my drink, I began laughing so hard. I loved how Shawna was just as blunt and in-your-face as I am! Then I tried to shake a really weird mental image out of my head while Ed and David continued the conversation.

"So what about the rest of it?" my husband asked.

"Oh, same room," Shawna said, jumping back into the

conversation. "Some couples will only play if they're in the same room with each other, as opposed to couples separating and playing in different rooms. We do same room until we get to know another couple pretty well and feel comfortable."

David nodded as I got my bearings. "What did Ed say about BDSM?"

His eyes flashed with a mischievous glint. "Oh, I travel with whips and chains on occasion." He winked at me. "Have you ever used a pair of nipple clamps? What about rope? I know some pretty knots."

"And I am really into girls, the more bi, the better, and bonus points if they're squirters," Shawna revealed.

"I haven't really thought much about being with a woman," I answered, though it wasn't apparent she was asking me. "I guess I won't know unless I try?"

"That's a good way to look at most anything in the life-style," Ed agreed, nodding his head.

"What's a squirter?" David asked.

Then I added, "Isn't that a myth? Like it's just pee or something?"

"Tell you what," Ed offered, "I'll let you watch me make Shawna squirt, and you can tell us if you think it's just pee." He winked at Shawna, who beamed without even a trace of embarrassment across her face.

After dessert, it was time to figure out our next step. "So do you guys want to come back to our house and test the waters?" Shawna asked. "We have a hot tub. We find that's a good way of 'dipping your toe in.'"

I looked at David, and he looked at me.

When neither of us jumped to answer, Ed took the

floor. "You know, the best piece of advice we could ever give is to make sure you are 100% on the same page before proceeding. And just because one of you is on one page tonight, it doesn't mean you're going to be the next night. It's always a good idea to keep the lines of communication clear and open. Transparency is an absolute must for this type of relationship to work," he advised.

"Trust me, we've had to work on our communication a great deal, and all that work has more than paid off. I feel closer to Shawna now than I ever have, more than I ever thought was even possible. We owe our great relationship to the lifestyle. It's brought out sides of us we never knew existed and has allowed us to be our most genuine selves with each other."

"Awww, Ed!" Shawna exclaimed, pulling his hand into hers on the tabletop and lacing their fingers together. "That is one of the sweetest things you've ever said!" She didn't blush when they were talking about sex or squirting, but her husband's declaration of devotion made her cheeks turn a rosy shade.

"What do you think the best way to get started is?" I asked. "If we agree to take the next step, I mean."

"Meeting us is a good first step," Shawna winked. "We have a pretty big community here in Sunview, and there are all types of events we could invite you to. There are house parties, meet and greets, and hotel takeovers. There's a club only an hour or so from here, too. It's a pretty tight-knit community, and you'll learn quickly enough that when you make lifestyle friends, they aren't just friends in the bedroom, but outside of it too. Lifestyle folks make the strongest, most loyal friends – "

"But what about what you said earlier? You know, about being careful and about drama?" I asked, hating to interrupt, but I was trying to reconcile what she was saying with what I heard earlier.

"Once you weed out the assholes," Ed explained, "what you're left with is the cream of the crop. Trust us on this!"

❧ 4 ❧

Ed and Shawna seemed so relaxed and comfortable in their circle of friends and with themselves. I wanted to skip ahead to that level of comfort. It seemed like it would be so much easier than being the newbies, the new kids on the block.

On the way back home, David and I agreed that we really liked them. We weren't 100% sold on getting into bed with them yet, but we felt that meeting them was a positive step in our journey.

"So what do we do next?" David asked as we crawled into bed. The babysitter had put the kids down at ten o'clock, as we'd suggested. "We can't get a sitter every single Saturday night, you know. That's going to add up fast!"

"You know, we could ask your parents to babysit. I thought part of the reason we moved here was to be closer to your parents."

My in-laws lived a couple of towns over, only about twenty minutes from us. It was not quite far away enough for my personal comfort, as they did tend to pop over a little too frequently for my tastes. It was the damn Lowes down the road from us. Their little town was smaller than Sunview and lacked some of the big box stores like Target and Lowes. So whenever they made shopping excursions. we'd often get phone calls with, "We're on our way over!" While it was nice to have a few minutes' notice, that's all it was, a few minutes. Barely enough time for me to sweep the proverbial dirt under the rug.

"Hot tub," I finally answered, breaking the silence after David didn't respond to my in-law babysitter comment.

"What?" he asked, turning toward me.

"Hot tub. We need a hot tub. Then we can invite people over here to play."

"But what about the kids?" he asked again.

"Don't we have other kids in our neighborhood? Couldn't we send them down the street to play?"

"All night?"

"However long it takes," I answered him with a wink.

ON MONDAY, I WAS GLAD TO ONCE AGAIN BASK IN THE beautiful quietness of my empty house. That meant no arguments over tater tots versus French fries, and no trying to bribe David to help me fold the laundry.

Note to self: blow jobs don't work anymore because he realizes I like to give them as much as he likes to get them.

My day stretched before me with gentle waves of peaceful bliss, and after I finished cleaning up the kitchen and posting my daily blog post, I could curl back up with my Kindle in my lovely reading nook.

Unless the doorbell rings, of course. And, obviously it did; otherwise I wouldn't be bitching about it.

"Mrs. Archer?" a man in a crisp navy blue uniform and matching hat asked. I squinted to make sense of the light-bulb-themed logo on his cap. *Anderson Electric*, it registered at last. He was a younger man with a closely-trimmed reddish-blond beard and a rich, golden tan that made his aqua blue eyes pop off his face.

My eyebrows furrowed, but not for long after my eyes wandered over his muscular body. "I am Mrs. Archer, but I didn't order an electrician," I finally answered, as a big gray cargo van pulled in next to the white Anderson Electric work truck.

"Mr. Archer hired us to run the electric for a new hot tub," the man in the uniform explained, tipping his hat at me and revealing straight white teeth emerging from plump lips. *Mmm, he can run my electric any time!* I thought to myself.

No sooner had I let him into the house (and checked out his ass as he made his way down the hall) did I have another uniformed man standing on my porch. He was dark-skinned with wide, chocolate-brown eyes and, I soon found out, a deep, rumbling voice. "Mrs. Archer?" he asked, his timbre like thunder. When I nodded he added, "I'm here to do the plumbing for your new hot tub."

I let the gray-uniformed plumber into the house, and he nodded to the electrician who was waiting for me between the living room and kitchen. I saw the plumber flash a look to the electrician, who gave him a cocky smirk. As I led them to the back of the house, I wondered if they were checking out *my* backside. From the weight of their stares, my guess was yes.

"I'm sorry, I don't think we've picked out a hot tub yet," I warned them. "And we haven't discussed where it will go."

"We have all the info we need right here," said the plumber in his rich, deep voice. He shot the electrician another look, then both men looked at me with easy, expectant grins.

I heard a scrape in the driveway as a truck lumbered onto the pavement before I could get another word off my tongue. The two men followed me back to the front door where we discovered a huge white delivery truck with "Sunview Pools & Spas" emblazoned on the side in a fancy, curlicue script. My heart began to pound against my ribcage as the realization of what was happening smacked into me. *Wow, just wow!* I could barely find any other words. David was just like this. He loved surprising me.

"Just sign here," the delivery driver said, brushing dark, wavy hair out of his eyes and handing me a clipboard. He was just as good-looking as the other two men, who turned to leave so they could get busy with their pipes and wires. The delivery driver wore black shorts revealing thick, bulging calf muscles and a slim-fitting red polo shirt. The bands on his short sleeves dug into his massive biceps as he took the clipboard from me and headed back to his truck with a smile creasing his gold-flecked eyes.

Is it bad that all I could think of was inviting all three of these gorgeous beasts into my bedroom for an impromptu gang-bang? I returned to my spot in the living room as the three men set about working to install our new hot tub. Before I picked my Kindle back up, I sent David a text thanking him with a bunch of heart and kiss emojis. *Where's the BJ emoji when you need it?* I wondered. If folding laundry didn't warrant a BJ, a new hot tub certainly did!

I picked up the Kindle so I could return to the steamy story I had started earlier that morning, but the sound of drilling distracted me. *Drilling...I wouldn't mind being drilled right now.*

Sometimes I swore I had the sex drive of a seventeen-year-old boy. David had acquiesced and gone down on me last night, gotten me off three times, and yet I still felt the need seizing up inside me, tingling in my groin and radiating from my core up to my nipples, which began to tighten as I imagined the three men working nearby becoming sympathetic to my plight.

I reached down and adjusted the short white tennis skirt I was wearing. *Hey, I don't play tennis, but this is my fantasy and that seems like the proper attire for a slutty housewife who is about to get it on with the electrician, plumber, and delivery driver.* I trailed a finger up my thigh, angling toward my clit, which was already pulsing with desire as my mind began to run away with the vivid fantasy it was creating.

"Excuse me, Mrs. Archer?" the electrician asked, peeking his head into the room. His eyes fell on my finger, which was hidden in the pleats of my tennis skirt, but so very obviously rubbing my clit as my eyes darted over the words in the erotic novel I was reading on my Kindle.

I could tell anything he was planning to ask me disappeared from the tip of his tongue as a hard bulge immediately began to grow between his legs. It was so obvious that seconds later when the plumber made his way into the room, he glanced at me first, and then his eyes immediately rocketed to the erection straining against the electrician's zipper, begging to be freed.

"Can we help you with something, Mrs. Archer?" the plumber managed to grunt out before his crotch met a similar fate. Sure enough, the delivery driver was next on the scene, and it only took him a once-over of the room to surmise what was going on.

"Oh, you are all so sweet to think about little old me," I sighed, selflessly pressing my fingertips to my chest as if I just couldn't fathom why I'd attracted their attention. "But, alas, I just returned from my tennis lessons, and I'm a bit.." As you know, women don't sweat; we merely glisten, so I finished the sentence with, "sparkly down there, if you know what I mean."

"You're sparkly up here, too," the delivery driver noted, as he leaned into the doorjamb, the mass of muscles in his arms tightening into thick, round bulges. I could only imagine how those arms would feel if he were on top of me, and I were flanked on either side by the other two men.

"Why don't we help you off with that skirt?' suggested the electrician, piercing me with his aqua eyes.

"And I could start the shower for you," added the plumber. "After all, hot pipes are my specialty."

"Well, aren't you all so gentlemanly!" I stood up from my perch, setting my kindle down on the sofa cushion. *Sometimes real life is stranger than fiction, or so they say.*

Three pairs of eyes glued themselves to my chest as I lifted my white tennis shirt over my head. My full, luscious breasts fell heavy into my wired push-up bra, my nipples pressing insistently against the white lace, begging for attention. Before I could reach around to unclasp it, the very attentive electrician had already stepped behind me to assist in its removal. *How thoughtful!*

He unhooked the clasps and pulled the lacy undergarment away from my skin. This time when my breasts fell, it was against my bare ribcage. Mr. Electrician was already working on my skirt, unbuttoning it and pulling the zipper down so that he could wiggle the fabric down my thick thighs. I watched the other two men as the skirt made its way to the floor, and they were both shifting uncomfortably as if their pants had suddenly grown too tight.

The plumber headed down the hall to the master bedroom, where he pushed open the door to the bathroom and turned on the shower. I heard the water hitting the tile as the other two gentlemen accompanied me into the bathroom. The plumber had taken the liberty of removing his clothes, and he stood before me, a fine male specimen, his muscles carved from sleek, dark marble, and his manhood jutting out proudly below his perfectly formed abs.

As if not to be outdone, the delivery driver stripped out of his shirt, revealing tightly coiled curls of chest hair springing up from two solid mounds of pectoral muscles. *Mmm...droolworthy*, I noted.

The electrician helped me into the shower as the steam began to rise up toward the ceiling. I felt the hot water cascade down my body, and even though it was quite warm, a shiver rocketed through me, budding my nipples so tightly I could have sworn they'd cut glass. This phenomenon did not escape the plumber's notice as he bent to swipe his warm tongue over the firm peaks.

Meanwhile, the delivery driver's shorts came off,

revealing his seriously muscular thighs and his swollen cock still straining against the fabric of his black boxer briefs. The electrician winked at me as he pulled his own shirt off, showing that his deep, golden tan extended past the confines of his clothing. He stripped out of his pants too, and sported a long cock with a meaty crown and a mess of reddish gold curls at the base.

Now I just needed to coax the delivery driver out of his boxer briefs, and I'd have three cocks staring at me with their greedy, hungry eyes.

It's a good thing we have a damn big shower because otherwise the four of us would not have fit. The plumber pulled me to his chest so that his cock pressed against my backside while the electrician dropped to his knees and parted my lips with his tongue. The delivery driver brushed his lips against the ones on my face as the water streamed down between us.

I couldn't believe I was letting three men have their way with me! And I wasn't even nervous. No, every nerve in my body was singing out with anticipation, with need.

All I wanted to do was come on each of their cocks over and over again as they took turns satisfying themselves with my (literally) dripping wet holes. And I kept thinking about David sneaking in to watch, stroking his cock as he witnessed three men enjoying his wife. Then, when everyone was gone, he could reclaim me, taking me every which way to re-establish that I belong to him.

The plumber reached behind himself to grab the pink loofah off the caddy that hung in the corner, and the delivery driver smiled as he poured a generous dollop of body wash onto it. My eyes opened just long enough to see the grin that spread across the plumber's face as he squeezed the mesh sponge repeatedly to form tiny, iridescent bubbles. Satisfied, he handed the sponge over to the delivery driver, who began to soap up my body with the sponge.

Not once did the electrician, whose face was still buried in my quivering sex, waver. He was fully dedicated to bringing me to orgasm, and my only fear was that I would slip and fall when it finally overcame me.

My thighs began to tremble as I neared the point of no return. My moans echoed over the sound of the shower beating down on the tile as the electrician took my clit into his mouth. My eyes flashed open for just a second, long enough to witness him take his throbbing-with-need cock into his fist and begin to stroke it up and down in an attempt to relieve some pressure. As soon as I came, I would beg him to slide it inside of me, to feel out how wet he made me—and not from the shower.

The muscles in my arms and legs tightened alongside the ones in my core as I ground my pussy into his face. I leaned back against the plumber, feeling his cock pierce the crack between the two globes of my ass. He held me against him, taking my weight as if he knew that in a few moments, I wouldn't be able to stand on my own. The delivery driver diverted his attention to my nipples, and I noticed he, too, was stroking his cock with long, sure strokes up and down this thick shaft as the water beaded on his neck and shoulders, cascading off his dark, wavy locks.

As teeth bit into my nipples, hands dug into the flesh of my hips, and strong arms lifted me, I began to unravel, like a tiny crack in a huge granite slab at first, until it rocketed through me like the space shuttle blasting off toward the heavens. I exploded between their bodies, cradled in their limbs, writhing against their faces and cocks and arms as I came in torrents, in waves of pleasure.

I began to resurface, the purple fading into the bright light of the day when my eyes fluttered open. I was dry, legs curled beneath me, my Kindle spread open next to me.

"Mrs. Archer?" I heard the deep voice of the plumber break me from the bubble I was trapped in.

"Yes?" *Oh, shit.* I must have drifted off.

"Come see your new hot tub!"

"WELL, WHAT DO YOU THINK?" DAVID ASKED, STRETCHING his arms out and pulling me closer to his body.

The jets spurted onto those spots in the small of my back that always seem to vex me, and the one right under my crotch was vaguely tickling my clit. I was a fan of the hot tub. No doubt about it. "Honey, this may be the best present you've ever gotten me!"

"Really?" His eyes lit up. He spoils me, so there have been many, many presents through the years. "Nothing but the best for my bride!" He leaned over to plant a kiss on my cheek, which was growing moist from the mist kicked up by the jets.

"Are you ready to share this baby with some hot life-style peeps?" I questioned, turning to face him. I pulled his hand into mine.

"Depends," he answered, raising a brow. "Did you find a babysitter for Saturday night?"

"I'm going to ask our neighbor Jenna if she'd mind keeping the kids."

"Jenna…?" he asked, his eyes drifting up to the clouds as if he was trying to place her.

We installed the hot tub on our patio so it was accessible from our walk-out basement. It was perfect. Now we just needed a fence on the other side of our property so people driving by couldn't see into our yard. The house next to us was on the market, and who knew what kind of prudes might buy it? There was already a fence between our properties, but I had a feeling it wasn't high enough to completely block the view. A nice, tall privacy fence around the entire perimeter of our yard would be a good, manly summer project for David and Aidan to bond over.

"I think you met Jenna when we first moved in? She's the cute single mom who lives two houses down from us."

"Cute single mom?" David's eyebrows shot up again.

"Yes…I think so, anyway. She seems…kinda innocent and…unassuming though," I added.

"Maybe she's a unicorn?" he guessed.

"A single bi female?" I laughed. "Yeah, what are the chances there are other swingers on Juniper Court?"

"Maybe you should ask her?"

"Like what, just go up to her and say, 'Hey, Jenna, just wondering, do you like girls?'"

"You're not exactly known for your subtlety, Valley. I can't see you asking her any other way than just blurting it right out."

I chuckled. *He knows me so well*, I thought as I stroked my hand down his thigh. If the kids weren't still awake, I'd certainly swing my legs over his hips and take a ride. It sucked that we had to wear swimsuits in our inauguration of the new hot tub. I couldn't wait to get in this thing and strip off our clothes. That would be when the real fun started!

"Hey, are you saying you want to see me with a woman?" I asked him, watching his face light up from the mere mention of the idea. Now even if he denied it, I'd know he was lying.

"Well...maybe..." He squeezed my hand just before it brushed against his cock. There was no doubt it was reacting favorably to the idea of seeing me with a woman.

"No, you have to really say it, David." I gave him a serious look, daring him to voice the words.

He leaned down into my face and whispered in my ear, "I'm dying to see you with a girl."

"I think we can arrange that," I answered and watched his cheeks spread with a devious grin.

♏ 5 ♌

I wasn't sure what the theme of Spring Fling meant, wardrobe-wise. I would have never pictured myself spending time in deep contemplation over what to wear to my first lifestyle house party, but here I am. I chose a long duster-style sweater over my short shorts and corset-style lace-up top, and naturally our neighbor got a glimpse of me when he was out walking his dog. I saw his eyebrows shoot up with interest, but I tried to pretend like I didn't notice. *Oy.*

David was like a remora suctioned to my side as we filtered through the crowd in the living room and kitchen. I guess that makes me the shark in this metaphor. *I'm good with that.* It just so happened that Ed and Shawna were hosting a house party and were happy to add us to the guest list. We were thrilled to learn that they knew pretty much everyone in the community. I felt like we'd hit the swinger jackpot!

As they gave us a tour of their home, they introduced us to so many couples and single men that I thought my head might explode trying to remember them all. There were people of all different sizes, shapes, races and ages, which was a relief. It was hard to get a good impression of the demographics from the swinger website because so many of the pictures were close-ups of naked bodies. I mean, all the boobs started to blend together after a while. It was really nice getting to put faces and names together from the get-go instead of wading through endless profiles and sending emails that often went unanswered. From what I understood, that was par for the course. This swinging thing was not a walk in the park. You really had to put some effort into meeting compatible partners.

I had told Shawna about some of my experiences with emails on the site. I told her I got several emails a day from couples, but when I wrote back, it always seemed to be just a man on the other end. And he'd say things like, "I'll check with my wife, but I'm sure she'd love to meet you." Shawna informed me that there was an epidemic of single men masquerading as couples on the websites, and that in many cases, there was, in fact, no wife waiting in the wings. She warned me to be extra careful and not to go through with meeting anyone until we had spoken to both parties.

"Oh, so that's why you wanted to talk to me too, not just David, before we met!" I realized.

"Yup! You're catching on," she replied, stroking her long, red, manicured fingernails down my dark hair affectionately.

I was trying to formulate a mental catalog of all the people I thought we might want to get to know better when we reached the hallway where all the bedrooms were located. I noticed they were all empty. "No one is fucking," I observed. "Why is no one fucking?" Disappointment echoed through my words.

Ed chuckled. "The party just started! Give everyone a chance to get some drinks in them and loosen up, and then these rooms will fill up. Trust me on this!"

"Loosen up?" I giggled with my eyebrow cocked. David just groaned at my dirty mind.

"Did you see anyone you were interested in?" Shawna asked. David and I both shrugged. "Have a few drinks; don't be afraid to strike up conversations and see where things go. You're a young, good-looking couple. You won't have any trouble attracting interest." She patted David on the back, then slid her hand down to squeeze his ass cheek. "Especially not with an ass like that, my dear!"

My husband did have a fine ass. There was no doubt about that. "So what happens when we find someone we want to play with?" I questioned.

"Simply ask them if they want to play. If they say yes, ask them what kind of rules or limits they have. Then find a place. That's about it. Oh, if the door to a bedroom is open, you can go right in. If it's closed, don't go in. Just make sure you ask before joining in any play in progress. The rules aren't really that complicated," she explained.

"And if anyone gives you any trouble, just let me know!" Ed added, taking a deep breath and puffing out his chest. "We want to make sure everyone feels comfortable and has a good time."

"Oh, there are condoms in every room and a stack of towels if you need them. Sheets in the linen closet in case there's a mess." She winked. "I've been known to soak a sheet or two in my day. We have plastic covers on all the mattresses." Ed laughed at his wife's admission.

I glanced at David, who was taking everything in as he always did. He was always able to maintain a poker face, and later he'd tell me his impressions of everything. I was more of a wear-my-heart-on-my-sleeve type person. It was almost impossible for me to conceal my thoughts about things. If I didn't just blurt out my feelings, then they were certainly reflected on my face for everyone to see. *Oh, well. No one could accuse me of being disingenuous, that's for sure.*

"Well, I'm sure there will be no shortage of couples who want to take your lifestyle virginity," Ed claimed. "Just go have fun!"

David gave him a curt nod and a handshake as if we had just completed a business transaction. I, on the other hand, threw my arms around them both and thanked them again for having us.

"Yeah, we aren't always so quick to invite newbies to house parties until we get to know them a little better," Shawna said. "But we have a good feeling about you two." She winked and then led Ed back into the kitchen. I felt like we'd just earned the official swinger gold seal of approval!

David and I found ourselves alone in the hallway, well away from the din of the party. It sounded like a bevy of new guests had arrived, and we heard their voices echoing from the foyer as they greeted everyone. "Shall we go be social?" I asked.

He smiled at me. "Yep, I'm ready."

"You're sure, right?" I verified.

"As ready as I'm ever going to be!"

I SAW THEM ON THE DECK BY THEMSELVES. THEY SEEMED TO be about our age, maybe a few years older, but definitely in their thirties. She had long, golden blonde hair that fell in soft waves around her bare shoulders. It blew in the breeze that rustled through the palms on that side of Ed and Shawna's yard. The moon was rising in the indigo sky and beaming down on her, nearly making her glow as she basked in its light. He was in a shadow, but when I moved closer, I noticed he was strikingly handsome, with dark hair, sideburns and thick, expressive brows that cocked as soon as his dark eyes caught sight of me.

I motioned for David, who was following behind me with fresh margaritas in his hands, to join me as I approached them. As soon as they realized we were coming their way, smiles curled the corners of their mouths. "Hi!" I broke the ice, turning to take my icy cold margarita from David and raising it toward them. "I'm Valley, and this is my husband David."

"Hi guys," the woman answered in a silky voice. "We're Hailey and Evan." She reached out to clink her glass with mine. "Cheers!"

David shook Evan's hand and then leaned in to give Hailey a kiss on the cheek. "It's nice to meet you. It's our first party," he admitted sheepishly.

I turned and shot him a tiny glare, then returned a glowing smile to our new friends. "Sorry, we're a little new at this. We just met Ed and Shawna last weekend!"

"Wow, that is new. Well, Ed and Shawna are the couple to know. They throw the best parties, so you're in good hands," Evan assured us.

"Absolutely! Did you meet them on LifestyleMeet or

through the Sunview Lifestyle Community Facebook group?" Hailey questioned.

"Facebook group?" I scoffed. "Really? Uh, no, the website. You guys meet people on Facebook?" I vaguely remembered Shawna saying something about that, but I must have blocked it out because it seemed so…outrageous.

My parents and in-laws are on Facebook. They stalk my page like…uh…stalkers, that's what. Not because they care about me. They just want to see photos of the kids. Still, there's no way we could participate in lifestyle stuff on Facebook.

Hailey laughed, and it was a sparkly golden arpeggio that reached a peak, then faded away like a star in the first light of morning. "We have…uh…I guess you could call it an alternative Facebook profile."

"Alternative?"

She nodded. "Yeah, it's called *FitCoupleForFun*, same as our username on the website. Helps us get to know people online before we meet at parties or for playdates or whatever. There are all sorts of groups on Facebook where we post pictures, parties, talk about lifestyle issues and all that."

"Oh, yeah," Evan jumped in. "I go on there solely for the photos. Tata Tuesday is my favorite!"

Hailey elbowed him in the ribs. "Only because I don't have much in the tata department." She giggled.

"Honey, your tits are perfect!" he retorted, reaching down to give them a squeeze. "You wanna see?" He raised his eyes to me as if he were directing the question my way.

"Uh…sure," I stammered, trying to reconcile the fact

that this guy just asked if I wanted to see his wife's boobs. It didn't seem like the kind of thing you should turn down at a swinger party.

David's eyes matched the moon in size as Evan hooked his finger beneath the elastic of his wife's simple, strapless dress and pulled it down. He revealed two small, perky, tan breasts with pink eraser-shaped nipples pierced with tiny silver barbells.

"Wow!" I gasped, immediately wondering what those barbells might feel like against my tongue. I had just taken a giant slurp of my margarita, which had gone straight to my head. Just before my hand impulsively reached out to cop a feel, I remembered what Shawna and Ed had said about asking first.

"Go on," Hailey encouraged me as if she could read my thoughts. "You can touch them."

I glanced over to David, who was nodding his head in agreement—no big surprise he was on board. I trailed my fingertips down the center of her chest, right between her small, firm mounds. She sighed as I took one of her hard nipples between my thumb and forefinger and gave it a tiny tug, resting the pads of my fingers against the metal balls on the ends of her piercing. She let a soft moan escape her lips as her back involuntarily arched.

"Damn, that's hot," Evan said, moving out of the way so he could help me maneuver closer to his wife.

She reached up to stroke my cheek, then tilted my chin down to hers. She was nearly my height in her heels, but I could tell without them she would probably only be 5'4" or so. She had a tight, toned body that skimmed the black fabric of her dress. I imagined what it would look like dropping to the floor to gather around her heels.

Before I knew it, she was leaning toward me to brush her lips against mine. I felt a bolt of electricity shoot down my spine as our lips connected. She was so soft, it felt like a whisper against my mouth.

She pulled me closer to her, threading her fingers into my silky black hair so she could deepen our kiss. Her velvety tongue stroked against mine as another moan escaped, vibrating right through me. David moved behind me, wrapping his arms around my waist and pulling my ass into him so I could feel his erection pressing into my soft flesh.

"I think you two need to get a room," Evan suggested, gesturing toward the house with his drink. He didn't wait for an answer; he just led the way.

Moments later, Hailey and I stood by the edge of the bed in an empty bedroom, her arms wrapped around me, running her hands up and down my ample curves. David and Evan were talking, but I could only make out a few words over Hailey's heavy breaths and wanton moans. I am fairly certain he said they only did soft swap, but I wasn't entirely sure. I didn't care at that point; I wanted to fulfill my husband's fantasy of seeing me with another woman, and I had found just the woman to do it with.

I pulled on Hailey's dress, which was elastic at the top, and easily glided it down her svelte body. She stood before me in nothing but a lacy black thong and strappy red stiletto sandals. *Wow. She was just wow.* I had never really considered myself bisexual or even attracted to women, but I guess I hadn't realized how soft her lips would feel against mine, or how delicious her spicy jasmine scent would be in my nose. It had infiltrated my senses, seeping in straight to my core, which was growing wetter by the second.

"Your turn," she said, wiggling out of the panties so that only the heels remained. She had a clean-shaven mound between her small, shapely thighs. I suddenly felt a little self-conscious about my generous curves, but Evan didn't give me a chance to worry about them for long. He stepped behind me and nuzzled his lips against my neck.

"My wife loves curvy women, and you're a goddess," he whispered into my ear, his hands sliding down to my corset top. He began to unlace me from the back, but I whipped around to stop him.

"Unhook the front," I instructed him.

As he went to work on the metal clasps that held my breasts captive high above my waist, pushing them almost to my collarbones, Hailey worked on my shorts. She reached around me to deftly unfasten them with her slim, nimble fingers. My hips are rather curvaceous, so I knew she wouldn't be able to pull them straight down. With a combination of a belly-dancing type move and her tenacity, they soon slid down my thighs until I could step out of them.

I wasn't wearing panties at all, so now that Evan had managed to slip my corset off, I was completely naked. I stepped out of my silver thong sandals and posed in my birthday suit while three pairs of eyes gently caressed my womanly curves.

I could get used to all of this positive reinforcement, I thought, reveling in their worship. I was so used to disdainful stares from jealous bitches; it was so nice to be appreciated for a change! And Hailey had nothing to be jealous of—she was secure in the fact she had a fucking amazing body too.

"My god, you are so gorgeous!" Hailey exclaimed before kissing me again. As our tongues danced together, her lips so soft they felt like clouds, her hands wandered down to cup my breasts. "They're so full, so heavy!" she gasped as she pulled away from me.

I wanted to see the expression on David's face, but before I could, she pushed me back onto the bed till I bent, my bottom hitting the mattress before I could voice any objections. Not that I would have objected, but there was no time, anyway. Evan asked if I wanted the door shut, but I wasn't able to answer because Hailey had captured my lips with her mouth again and was grinding her tight little body into mine.

She pulled away just long enough to pant, "Can I lick your pussy?"

Who am I to say no to an offer like that?

Hardly waiting for a reply, she slid down my body, still gasping for air. I felt the bed shift as both Evan and David took a seat on either side of me, eagerly awaiting the next act of the theatrical production we were staging. While Hailey made herself comfortable nestled between my thighs, I glanced up long enough to notice we'd attracted a wider audience gathered by the door.

Hailey's sparkling blue eyes flashed up at me just before her tongue delved out to flick against my swollen clit. I nearly jumped out of my skin, the sensation was so intense. She gave my clit a light, delicate tongue-lashing that had me bucking against her, silently begging for more as my eyes snapped shut and my hips writhed against the sheets. I could tell she had done this a time or two. I wondered if I would be able to adequately return the favor.

I had never really thought about going down on a woman before... Would she like the same things I like? Would she want it gentle or rough? Would she want my fingers inside her, curling against her G-spot?

No sooner had the thought formed in my mind that she seemed to read it. She pulled up to shoot me a fiery look of desire as she stroked her tongue against two of her fingers, wetting them with the mixture of saliva and my juices that spilled from her mouth. She reached down and swiped her fingers between my slit, parting my lips easily with her moistened digits. One, then two fingers slid inside me as I gasped, pleasure rocketing through me as she instantly found my G-spot.

"Fuck," I moaned as she drilled them inside me, hitting the perfect spot with every thrust. Once she was satisfied she had found my hot button, she returned her tongue to my clit. The intensity of her strokes on my clit and inside me had me climbing the cliff to an orgasm in no time, but I suddenly wanted to taste her too. I reached down and grabbed her head, pulling her back to look at me.

"What's wrong?" she questioned, worry furrowing her brows.

"Flip around so we can sixty-nine," I directed her. A wicked grin lit up her face as she eagerly complied, shifting herself around on the bed so she could straddle me, gently lowering her pulsating pussy toward my face.

I could smell her before I tasted her, the wild jasmine scent filling my nose again as the heat of her desire began to radiate toward me. I tipped my tongue up to catch her lips, the shock of her honey sweetness tearing through my taste buds. I couldn't believe how sweet she tasted. I had never sampled another woman except for myself, and that was usually only on David's lips or sometimes on his cock if I went down on him after he'd been inside me. But it was always diluted with his musky scent. This was pure, unadulterated woman sizzling on my tongue, filling my whole being with her heady perfume.

A deep growl vibrated through the room as her pelvis sank down toward my face. I placed my hands on the taut globes of her ass, pushing my tongue deeper inside her as she began to once again lap away at my throbbing clit. I was trying to hold back at this point. I wanted to catch her up to where I was so we could orgasm together. I wasn't confident I'd be able to concentrate on licking her once my orgasm struck. It would be like trying to run and swim all at the same time.

Fortunately, focusing on establishing a rhythm as I nipped and sucked at her clit helped keep me from falling off the cliff. The way she dug her hips into me was so fucking erotic, though. I wished I could have seen David's expression while she fucked my face; I just knew he was sporting a raging boner as he witnessed the show.

"God, you're really good at this," she finally gasped, breaking away from my clit. Her words were garbled against my wet folds. "I'm gonna come!" The last word came out almost as a howl as she rocked against me.

For a moment I wasn't sure if I was going to have enough oxygen to survive as she grabbed ahold of my legs and buried her face in my pussy like her life depended on making me come too. Feeling her spasm against my lips drove me over the edge, and in a burst of lightning, I was bucking into her face as wildly as she was bucking into mine.

For several glorious seconds we were suspended in some sort of glittering freefall while our bodies rode wave after wave of pleasure. When I finally came to and she rolled off me and into her husband's waiting arms, David was there to scoop me into his own.

"That was the hottest fucking thing I've ever seen," he said, and he didn't waste any time unzipping his pants. He bent me over the bed and took me right there, while our audience appreciatively continued watching the spectacle.

❧ 6 ❧

There's nothing like a Spring Carnival at your kids' school to make the reality of your life sink back in. All week long I had been riding the high from the party the weekend before, until Wednesday night crept up on me like a ninja. I was completely oblivious to the whole carnival thing, too, until Aidan asked, "Is that what you're wearing to the carnival?"

I looked down at my fraying cut-off denim shorts that just barely cover my thighs. On top I was wearing a spaghetti strap cami that, if I wasn't careful, could shift at any moment and expose the cups of my black lace bra. *Oops.* It was just so freaking hot out! And our neighbor across the street, Greer, is such a hottie. I was outside all afternoon waiting for him to notice me as he mowed his lawn, but he never did. *Sigh.*

There is something to be said for the liberation I have felt the past few weeks since we embarked upon this whole lifestyle thing. David will tell you I have always been a tremendous flirt. No wonder I don't think women like me. Their husbands flirt with me; I flirt back. It's like I can't even stop myself.

Now, it's not like I would ever hurt anyone's marriage. I wouldn't fucking do that. I'm not a homewrecker, and flirting is harmless. But knowing there are couples out there who are open to it—well, it's just the ultimate sense of freedom. I wish I could explain it better. I feel like a lonely, horny bird who lived in a cage her whole life and then was suddenly set free, just in time to discover a whole bunch of horny birds just like her.

"Oh, shit, that's tonight?" I gasped, looking up from the pot where I was boiling spaghetti.

Aidan rolled his eyes at my use of an expletive and nodded emphatically, pointing to the calendar on the refrigerator where it said CARNIVAL in big red block letters. I've never been one of those moms who can go from swearing like a sailor when their kids aren't around to channeling their inner June Cleaver when they are. *I'm just Valley all the time. Take it or leave it.*

"I thought we were going to eat dinner there?" Aubrey said, joining us in the kitchen. She was wearing a sweet yellow floral sundress with a smocked top and cap sleeves and looked absolutely adorable. She was such a little lady sometimes that I wondered how she could truly be my child. Her hair was still in two long, dark braids and not a strand was out of place. When I was seven, if my mom sent me to school in braids, I'd return home with chunks falling out and wisps framing my face haphazardly.

"Oh, god, you're right. And I'm signed up to help out with face painting from 6-7." I glanced up at the clock on the kitchen wall. It was 5:30. *Shit. Where is my husband?* I wondered. I thought he was going to be home by 5:00.

As if on cue, the garage door squeaked open. I looked at the kids for a second, who were both wearing expectant looks on their faces that seemed to say "Adult-up, Mom!" I ran down the hall to our bedroom and began the process of trying to find something semi-conservative in my wardrobe, an outfit that would avoid the glaring stares of all the prim and proper PTA moms.

David wandered into the bedroom about the time I was standing in my bra and panties (*yes, I do wear them on occasion*) in front of my closet with a look of frustration painted on my face. I was waiting for the appropriate outfit to just leap out at me.

He approached me from behind and wrapped his arms around me, nuzzling into my neck so that his warm breath fell on my skin. I felt my nipples harden as his lips pressed into that delicate space where my neck meets my shoulder. *Oh, fuck...who cares about the carnival? Maybe we could stay home and fuck instead?*

I turned around to greet him, my lips finding his in a flash. I loved the way his arms tightened around me, pressing me to his body as if he never wanted to let me go. It was amazing how we could say so much to each other without speaking a word. *This man is my everything.*

I know if I were to tell anyone about my fantasies of fucking other men, the first thing they would assume is that I don't love my husband. That couldn't be further from the truth. I love this man as though his soul is my own. It may be that our souls are impossibly entangled. I have known him and loved him for so long now, I can't imagine not being his, not being bound to him.

My sexual fantasies have nothing to do with my feelings for David. They have everything to do with desire.

He makes me feel safe and secure enough to explore my fantasies. He wants to do it with me. That makes me love him all the more.

"How was your day, honey?" he asked, pulling away from our embrace.

"We have to be at the kids' school in less than thirty minutes for the Spring Carnival," I replied, breaking from my trance that led me to believe we had all the time in the world. Shit, I had been wardrobe contemplating and we had been kissing long enough that we lost five minutes. "Make that twenty-five minutes."

"Shit. That thing is tonight?"

See? I'm not the only one who forgot. We are the best parents, I swear. "Yep. And I can't find anything motherly to wear."

He chuckled as he peeked into my closet. "How about this?" he asked, pulling out a shirt. It was sleeveless with a high neck, though it was cut out on the shoulders so I would have to wear a strapless bra. It was a nice, neutral beige color with a brown and peach geometric design. It actually sounds quite ugly to describe it now, but trust me, it was probably the least offensive thing in my entire closet.

"Yeah, okay, with my khaki cargo capris. That could work," I said, taking the shirt from him and sliding it over my head. "You better change too, unless you want to wear the shirt and tie."

"Oh, hell no." He immediately began to strip, and I had to turn away. If I saw his sexy body naked, I might be forced to jump his bones. And then we'd never get to the carnival on time.

I DON'T KNOW HOW I COULD DESCRIBE THE FEELINGS filtering through me as I made my way through the crowd at my kids' school. As I headed to the face painting booth for my 6-7 PM shift, I passed some of the many moms who've given me the stink eye so far this school year. I knew one, Mrs. Emily Walters, was the PTA president and the mother of the smartest kid in Aidan's fifth grade class. Every time he brought home a test with an A on it and I congratulated him, he always said something to the effect of, "Ava still scored better than me."

I had tried to console him the best way I knew how. I told him he was only competing against himself, and that you couldn't do better than an A. And he would say things like "But Ava got an A+." And I would say, "Who cares what Ava got?" And Aidan would say, "I got beaten by a girl again."

"Whoa, whoa, whoa," I had protested. "What does that mean? Beaten by a girl?"

"Girls aren't supposed to be so good at math," he replied.

As you can imagine, my hackles were instantly raised. "Who told you that?"

I knew David would never say such a thing. He would be too afraid I'd beat him up (lol). So he had to be getting that from some other source, most definitely outside our home.

"Oh, Mr. Snyder says it every day in math. Everyone laughs like it's a big joke."

"What do you mean, he says it every day?"

Aidan had shrugged. "Well, maybe not every day. Like twice a week, probably."

I had half a mind to call the principal up to say something. I might very well do that, as a matter of fact, and seeing Mrs. Walters reminded me. I doubt she would take too kindly to her straight A-earning daughter being fed that line of bullshit in her math class by her male teacher.

Once Emily's eyes connected with me, though, I froze. She was wearing prim little denim jumper with pastel flowers embroidered across the peter pan collar. *Who the hell wears denim jumpers?* I wondered. I felt like I had stepped in a time machine and been transported back to 1985, or maybe it was 1885. Her hair was permed in tight, auburn spirals, and she had glasses perched on her little upturned nose. I looked down at my khaki cropped pants and conservative shirt, even though, yes, my shoulders were showing, but it was already 85 degrees out at the beginning of May.

"Mrs. Archer!" she exclaimed. "We haven't seen you at any of the spring PTA meetings."

I felt like if she had a ruler on her, she might ask me to stretch my hands out so she could rap me across the knuckles à la a Catholic school nun. Maybe the denim jumper was the secular version of a habit?

"Oh, gosh, I'm sorry. I've been so busy, I—"

"I didn't think you worked outside the house," she retorted, her eyeballs shooting little fiery daggers at me.

"I, uh—well—"

"And your two children are both in school all day, are they not?" She took a deep whiff of indignation and stood with a fist pressed against her hip.

"Well, I've been slowly getting myself back into the

workforce…reading up, you know. Oh, and I have a blog. Not sure if you knew that—I blog about interior design."

"Oh!" Her eyes brightened. "Interior design! Well, you might be a real asset to our team that's in charge of the school media center remodel this summer. The school got a really wonderful state education department grant—which I wrote, because that's what I do, you know. I'm a grant writer. I've been awarded over eight million dollars in grants—and counting!"

She paused ever-so-briefly as if she expected me to start a standing ovation in praise of her outstanding success. If anyone needed a standing ovation, it was me for not allowing my internal eye roll to become an external one. But there was no time for that because she continued to fucking brag about how awesome she is.

"With the grants I've secured and my husband being president of the school board, we've been responsible for most of the wonderful improvements that have been made to Sunview Community Schools. Of course, this grant was only for twenty thousand, but with that we can upgrade some of the computers, take up the old carpeting, and get some new shelving and seating and all that. I'm sure you would LOVE to donate your interior design expertise to the cause, wouldn't you?"

"I…uh…well…" I wanted to smack my bumbling ass upside the head. Why couldn't I manage to say that word which I heretofore had never had any problems saying? The N-O word. NO! What the flipping hell was my problem? Apparently all my strength was wasted on preventing that massive eye roll.

All I could hear was David's voice echoing in my head.

Couldn't you at least TRY to make friends, Valley? Try to fit in? It would mean so much to the kids. We've been here nine months now, and you don't have any female friends in the area, and our kids haven't been invited to ONE party or sleepover since we moved.

That whole maternal guilt thing is a pretty fucking strong force. It overcame me so thoroughly, so powerfully that I just smiled and nodded at Mrs. Walters' request. *How could her face look any more pleased and smug all at the same time?* I wondered.

"I'll be in touch with you, Valley," she promised, the words spit out from behind her clenched teeth. Maybe she had expected me to say no? "I'll be in touch."

It had a pretty ominous ring to it.

AS WILLING AS DAVID WAS TO TRY SWINGING, I FELT A SENSE of obligation to try making some "vanilla" friends. We learned from Ed and Shawna that non-swingers were "vanilla," you know, like plain, unadorned, dull ice cream. But the fitting-in thing seemed to be looking up. At least in the neighborhood.

Aidan ran into the house on a Saturday morning as if he'd been chased by a bear. "Whoa, slow down!" I admonished him as he slid toward the refrigerator. It looked like he was sliding into home plate.

"Sorry, Mom; I gotta get back out there!" He panted as he stabbed his Capri Sun with the pointed plastic straw and brought it to his mouth.

"What's going on?"

"We're playing light sabers! We're going to have a

battle!" he cheered. Clearly it was the most exciting thing to happen in his young life thus far.

"Who's 'we?'" I questioned, knowing that his sister, girly-girl that she was, abhorred anything to do with *Star Wars*.

"Our neighbors!"

"Neighbors?" My ears totally perked at the word. "Which neighbors?"

"I met some cool kids when I rode my bike around the cully sack."

"Cul-de-sac," I corrected him."

"Whatever. They live in the big gray house with black shutters on the other side." There were only seven houses on Juniper Court. I went through my mental catalog until I matched it with the name of the family who lived there.

"Oh, the Garrett boys?" I squinted as if that would help me conjure up an image of them and their mother.

"Van and Shane," he told me.

I nodded. Their mom, Posey, was the widow who lived in #57. It was terrible what happened to her husband. I didn't know until we'd been here a month or two. The neighbor Jenna from a couple houses down told me. He was a cop, killed in the line of duty. So sad. I had gotten to know Posey a little bit at a few of the neighborhood functions I'd been to. A while back I'd gotten her an appointment with my hairdresser. So, see, maybe I was making friends after all?

"Okay, honey, have fun. Oh, and maybe you could ask their mom if she minds if you stay at their place next Saturday night? Your dad and I have a work function to attend and will be out late."

Work function? Did I just lie to my kid?

There was no work function. The only thing happening the following weekend was dinner with the couple we'd met at Ed and Shawna's party, Evan and Hailey. Even though David had warned me they were a soft swap couple, I was hoping in the heat of the moment, they'd change their minds.

Hey, it's okay to fantasize, right?

"ANYTHING GOOD?" DAVID ASKED AS HE LEANED OVER MY shoulder. I was sitting in his office chair, hunched over the laptop as if I were examining highly classified documents.

"We've got some mail!" I cheered as the icon danced in front of me. When I clicked on the inbox, three messages were bolded to indicate they were new.

I clicked on the first one and immediately rolled my eyes.

"U guys seem cool. Can I C ur pics?" it asked.

"What? That's it?" David complained.

I clicked on the profile, and it was just the lower half of an abdomen along with an erect penis and set of fleshy, low-hanging balls. *Ick.* Note to men who want to show off their junk on websites: at least have something nice to look at. They always say to put your best foot forward, but if this was the dude's "best foot," I'd hate to see what his worst one looked like!

"It would have taken *so* much effort to spell all those words out," David observed, shaking his head. "I'd venture that any guy not willing to spell out the word 'see,' probably takes plenty of other shortcuts too."

I nodded in agreement, then went on to the next item in our inbox. It was a couple this time, and their message was polite and to the point: "Greetings from Madison Heights. We see you're not too far away from us in Sunview. We have a condo there and visit most weekends. Any chance of meeting for dinner and seeing where it goes?"

David's eyebrow rose curiously as I clicked on their profile picture. What I saw made me want to find the nearest bottle of bleach to obliterate the image from my memory. It was a couple, probably in their fifties, which was fine, but the man had a thick neck ringed with gold chains, a flabby, hairy torso, and the *pièce de résistance* was a rather greasy mustache perched on top of his lips like a New York city sewer rat. And that was it. The picture only went from his nose to his gut. No eyes, no package, just mustache to navel. *What the hell?*

His partner in crime wore a flimsy, sheer red negligee trimmed in matching marabou. She had large, pendulous, sagging breasts and a fleshy, dimpled midsection. She was smiling wide enough to reveal yellow, crooked teeth poking out from her thin lips.

"Oh no," David gasped as if he didn't know what else to say.

I was right there with him, but too afraid anything I said might be misconstrued as elitist—or just plain mean. After all, they did seem very nice in their message, and their profile was equally articulate. But...but these were not people I could even remotely imagine getting naked with.

"I just—" I began, but then stopped as I racked my brain for something nice to say.

"It's a no from me," David said, doing his best Simon Cowell impression.

That was when I just erupted in laughter. It spilled out of me with such force and vivacity that David was compelled to slap his hands over my mouth. "Don't wake the kids!" he chided me as the laughter continued to bubble out against his palms.

The simple fact that the two of us were huddled around a laptop looking at profiles on a swinger site was suddenly beyond absurd to me. I felt like a character in one of those romance novels I read all the time, only this was even more outrageous than any of the crazy situations the heroines seemed to find themselves in.

"I'm sorry; I'm sorry," I finally gasped, trying to rein in my amusement. "Let's see what's behind Door #3, shall we?" I tried to calm myself down, but my chest was still heaving with laughter as I clicked on the final new message in our inbox.

"What a lovely profile you have," David began to read aloud. "I travel to Sunview on business at least once per month, and I'd love to have some local friends to spend time with when I'm in town. You two look like just my type, and may I say the Mrs. is absolutely stunning! Please let me know if you'd like to get to know each other. Yours truly, Derek."

Well, my interest was certainly piqued, and even more so once I clicked on his username *AllAboutHer* to scope out his profile. He had opened his private photos for us, and the album was filled with images of a sleek, muscular physique, deliciously dark skin, and capped off with a perfectly sculpted face and soulful brown eyes.

I turned to look at my husband, whose brows were

furrowed. *Uh oh.* I sensed I couldn't act overly interested. "What do you think, honey?" I questioned, tossing the ball in his court.

He squinted at the photos again. "I don't think he's my type!" He laughed as if he'd just told the funniest joke ever.

"I think he may be *my* type," I admitted, trying to muster up a combination of nonchalance and sheepishness. "You wouldn't be opposed to a threesome, would you?" I searched his face for signs of his true feelings in advance of his verbal answer.

He pursed his lips as he studied my gaze, which was as neutral as I could make it. Inside, though, I was already envisioning having those dark, muscular limbs wrapped around me as I rode him to ecstasy. *Hey, what can I say?* I have a vivid imagination thanks to all those smutty novels I read.

"I'm not opposed," he finally answered. "As long as you're willing to return the favor."

I felt the excitement course through me as my fantasy expanded to include an image of David watching from the side of the bed, stroking his cock as he watched me being taken by another man. Now that was fucking hot, especially if it turned him on to watch.

"Of course I am, my dear. I didn't have any issues getting down and dirty with Hailey the other night, did I?"

His lips stretched into a grin. "Why no, no you did not." He pulled my hand toward his crotch, where his erection was immediately evident. "I have pretty fond memories of that night…"

"Oh, do you now?" I questioned, my green eyes

piercing into him. "Why don't you tell me what you remember?"

"I'd be happy to, provided you're on your knees sucking this huge boner you just gave me," he retorted, guiding me down to the floor between his legs.

"Mmmmm," I answered as he undid the fly on his pants. "Just let me lock the office door first…"

I SMILED WARMLY AT MY WIDE-EYED NEIGHBOR JENNA AS she let me into her house. She seemed surprised to see me, but before I could even get a word out of my mouth, she started to interrogate me.

"Did I hear right that you blog about interior design?" she asked. I thought I was there to ask her to babysit Aubrey; I wasn't expecting *her* to ask *me* questions.

"Oh, yep, sure do. My blog is called Valley Archer Design. I have a website," I answered as I glanced around her home. It was neat and plain, a little old-fashioned, but still cozy. "I do a lot of product reviews and that sort of thing."

"I thought so. That's really cool!" She blushed a little and twisted her long, dark ponytail between her fingers. "Emily Walters from the PTA was talking about you at our yoga class the other morning. She said you'd agreed to help out with the project to revamp the media center. And, well, I might have stalked you a little bit online after that…"

Her voice trailed off as if she couldn't believe she was admitting to something so embarrassing. I kept a smile plastered to my face, my lips frozen in their curled-up position. I don't mind being stalked. But I got a little tingle down my spine at the realization that countless people might be stalking the naked pics of me on the swinger site right at that very moment. Having my blog stalked seemed pretty trivial—not to mention innocent—by comparison.

"Are you involved with the PTA project too?" I questioned, hoping to bring the conversation back around to her. I needed to find a way to subtly ask her what she was doing on Saturday night, though, as David had so rightfully pointed out, I wasn't exactly gifted in the subtlety department.

"Oh, yeah, I guess I'm pretty much expected to, being a teacher and all. Not sure what help I will be, but I'll try. That Emily Walters can sure be persuasive," she said with a sigh of resignation. "Can I get you something to drink?"

There was something so old-fashioned and proper about her, even though I could have sworn she was younger than me. Maybe because she's an elementary school teacher, I don't know. "Oh, I'm fine, thanks. Where are your girls today?" I asked.

Jenna had twin daughters who were ten years old. It was a bit of a long shot asking her to keep Aubrey, who was three years younger, but maybe they'd all get along great? It would be like having a little sister for a night. Coming from someone who's had a little sister my whole life, having one for a night would be a breeze.

"They're with their dad, but they'll be back soon," she answered as if the topic was so unpleasant, she didn't want to speak of it any longer than necessary.

"Oh, I see." I didn't consider the fact her ex might have

them over the weekend, which would completely foil my plans.

She continued to stare at me expectantly, batting her eyelashes. She was very pretty; I couldn't deny that. But she didn't look like she had a naughty bone in her body. She probably wasn't into women. *Should I ask her?* I wondered if she would just let me watch while David fucked her? *Oh, shit.* Is it inappropriate to have thoughts like that about your neighbor? Particularly your same-sex neighbor? *Oh, well, it's not like I'd ever censored my thoughts before. I sure as hell wasn't going to start now.*

"I just wondered if your girls would be around this weekend? You see, my husband has a work function, and I've been having a hard time finding a sitter for Aubrey. Aidan is going to go hang out with the Garrett boys, and I wondered if—"

"Oh, you need me to keep her for the night?" Jenna asked, her face brightening. I nodded eagerly as she launched into a litany of things the girls could do at a sleepover together: popping popcorn, watching scary movies, painting each other's toenails, doing each other's hair, baking cookies. She concluded by saying, "A slumber party would be so much fun!"

Oh, sure, she was thinking of a slumber party for little girls. *But what could be more fun than a slumber party for adults?*

❧ 7 ☙

"**S**o, did you confirm everything with Evan and Hailey?" David asked as he loosened his tie.

I nodded and reached out to help him unbutton his shirt. He shrugged away from me and turned toward the closet. *Grrr. How am I supposed to jump his bones if he keeps walking away from me?*

"And you've made arrangements for the kids?" he questioned, returning his gaze to me.

"David, of course I have made all the arrangements. When have I ever dropped the ball when it comes to us going out for the night?"

He sighed. "I'm sorry; I guess I'm just a little nervous. Probably just left over nerves from my presentation to the church board today."

"How did it go?" I had been a little miffed that David had to work on a Saturday, which meant I had to shuttle the kids to their soccer games by myself that morning, then play the highly despised role of soccer mom around the rest of the uptight female suburbanites of Sunview.

They were all decked out in their LuLaRoe while I sat there with a cleavage-baring bright red off-the-shoulder top and stonewashed denim miniskirt. *Take that, soccer moms!* But I knew this presentation was beyond important to him. I already had some ideas about how to spend the haul he'd get from such a big project.

"It went really well," he smiled and leaned down to kiss me on the cheek. "I think they liked my designs, and they are going to meet to go over them this week, then let me know after that what tweaks they'd like to make."

"But you're definitely doing the project, right?" I verified. I didn't want to see the dollar signs flash before my eyes if there was any chance they were only a mirage.

"Definitely. Bill says everyone loves my work and they can't imagine any other architect on the job!"

"That's awesome, honey! See, I knew you didn't have anything to worry about," I said, stroking my hand down his arm.

He kissed me again, this time on the lips. "Thank you for all your support and cheerleading, sweetheart."

"Mmm, I think I need a better thank you kiss, baby," I goaded him as I pulled him closer to me by the shirt collar.

He chuckled under his breath as he began to peel the shirt from his body. I thought that meant we were going to pre-game it before our date with Evan and Hailey, but then he paced over to his closet to grab a different shirt, this time a black short-sleeved golf shirt.

"So how does this thing work tonight?" he asked as he pulled it over his head.

"I guess like our dinner with Ed and Shawna, only hopefully this time there will be an after party." I winked at him as I perused the top of my dresser for the jewelry I wanted to wear with my little black dress. I thought about wearing something flashier, but you couldn't go wrong with a classic LBD, right? Besides, this one hugged my curves like it was nobody's business and had a deep, plunging V neckline that showed the girls off to perfection.

I made the mistake of stepping outside earlier to call for Aidan and Aubrey to come inside, and Sully's eyes nearly popped out of his skull. *How does he have a knack for being outside every single time I venture out?* I certainly wasn't expecting the neighbors to be this nosy when we first moved to Juniper Court. Maybe we needed to move someplace with bigger lots if we got serious about this lifestyle business.

"Are we inviting them here or going to their place?"

"I thought we'd invite them here. After all, that's the reason I made sure the kids could stay over at the neighbors'. I want to put that hot tub to good use," I answered. Then my nose wrinkled up as I considered how awkward it would be—if things were really heating up—to climb out of the hot tub and come all the way upstairs to our bedroom to take things to the next level.

"So are we going to use our bedroom or what?" David asked as though he was reading my mind.

Our basement was quite the cozy, comfortable den at the present moment. We had a fully stocked bar down there, a half bath, and a theater set up with a loveseat and a row of actual crushed velvet theater seats that we nabbed when the old cinema in downtown Sunview finally remodeled. He had done the new design, of course. That was his first project when we moved here.

Now I heard compliments about how amazing the new movie theater was every time I was in the vicinity. Everyone loved the reclining seats and all the other amenities, not to mention the sleek, modern design. The old crimson velvet seats looked nice in our media room with its huge projection screen. We even found an old-fashioned popcorn popper to put down there.

But there was no bed and no real couch, just the small, cramped loveseat. There was a little ice cream parlor table and chairs near the bar area, and of course the four stools at the bar. But there was no place to FUCK. Clearly an oversight on my part.

"I guess we'd have to," I answered as my mind spun with lavish visions of a totally redesigned space, one that would be perfect for intimate gatherings and for larger lifestyle soirees like the one Ed and Shawna had hosted. Now that we had invested in the hot tub, it would be crazy not to use it for its intended purpose: to lure like-minded folks into our bed.

"But?" he questioned, his eyes darting between mine, because he knows just from the tone of my voice I have some reservations.

"Well, we're probably jumping the gun for tonight because who says we'll even make it to the bedroom?" I point out. "I mean, they are soft swap, after all. I didn't even touch Evan last time, and you didn't touch Hailey."

"I know, but it seems like we all hit it off so well. You never know what might happen in the hot tub –"

"True, but I just don't want to have too high of expectations. I guess if things progressed, we'd get out of the hot tub and go upstairs." It just seemed a lot more realistic —not to mention convenient—if we never had to leave the basement. If only the basement were more conducive to swinger activities…

David watched my face light up as soon as it hit me. Of course, it all made perfect sense.

"What is it, Valley?" His eyebrows were cocked as he waited for my brilliant idea to be revealed.

"We need to transform our basement into something more lifestyle-friendly," I suggested. "You know, with a bedroom and a full bathroom."

"That sounds like a major project," he said, trying to wrap his head around it. I know how much he hates when I get these bees in my bonnet that basically amount to putting him to work. But hey, with his background as an architect and mine as an interior designer, it would be wasting a lot of talent not to put our skills to good use right inside our own home. *Am I right or what? Come on, I'm always right.*

"It would be a major project, but think of how nice it would be to get out of the hot tub and right into bed? And then to have a shower right there to clean up afterwards?" I coaxed a smile out of him when I wrapped my arms around his neck and planted a soft kiss on the edge of his lips.

"And we already have the bar, so we just need more seating and—"

"How many bedrooms did Ed and Shawna have available for play at their house?" he asked, his face starting to light up with his own ideas.

"I think there were three, maybe four."

"Okay, so right now if we hosted a party, the only places people could really play are our room and the living room. And I guess the hot tub, but—"

"What are you thinking?" I searched his face for the answers, trying to find a clue in his eyes.

"Our basement is only half-finished. There's that whole other room where the hot water heater and furnace are and where we have all the storage and my little makeshift workshop..." His voice trailed off as if he was waiting for me to catch his drift.

"You want to finish the rest of the basement with individual bedrooms?" I guessed.

"Well, it would be one hell of a space for a lifestyle party, right?"

His eyes were dancing with excitement. I thought I'd have to really sell him on the idea, but it turned out we were on the same page as usual. "It wouldn't just be one hell of a space," I answered. "It would be like a swinger paradise!"

I watched Hailey daintily stab her fork into a tomato slice in her salad and then instantly regretted ordering the filet mignon. I'm not so much into the whole deprivation thing, if you hadn't already guessed. *I figure if I want a steak, I'll order a damn steak.* Maybe she just really enjoyed lettuce, who knows? But I did feel like somewhat of a clod stuffing my face with a big hunk of meat prior to getting it on with these people.

Evan's eyes kept darting over to mine through the whole dinner. Most of the interaction at the party we'd attended together at Ed and Shawna's had been between me and Hailey. I hardly remembered Evan laying a finger on me. I definitely hoped we could rectify that oversight sometime in the course of the evening.

"Dessert?" questioned our perky, red-haired waitress when she arrived back at our table. Evan's eyes immediately flicked to mine, and I felt his foot swipe against mine under the table.

"Oh, I couldn't possibly," Hailey sighed, pushing her half-eaten salad toward the edge of the table. "I'm just stuffed."

Oh, brother. My eyes wanted to roll so badly that I almost had to reach up and hold them in place with my fingers. "We'll just take the check please," I spoke up, hoping it would distract my eyes from their natural tendency to flip.

"Separate or together?" she questioned, her eyes flitting from mine to David's to Evan's. I noticed she didn't even look at Hailey.

I couldn't help but snicker as I thought of the alternative question: *same room or separate?* "Separate," I clarified, giving her a forced smile.

"Oh, allow me," Evan said. "Just one check."

The waitress hurried away as I shot him a surprised look. "Why wouldn't we split it?"

Hailey stared down at her half-full glass of wine as Evan's cheeks spread with a grin. "My wife said no one has ever eaten her pussy so well... It's the least we can do!" Sure enough, a blush crept across her face.

Damn! That was my first time, too, I thought, mentally patting myself on the back. "Maybe you should let David have a turn," I pointed out. "I think his skills are way better than mine."

"Is that so?" Evan questioned, just as the waitress

returned with the slim black folder containing our check. He reached behind him to retrieve his wallet from his back pants pocket. In a flash, he was sliding a platinum credit card into the slot inside the folder. The waitress picked it up with a smile and disappeared again.

"You should come back to our place," David suggested. "We have a brand new hot tub we'd like to christen."

"Well, how can we say no to that, right, honey?" Evan answered, looking over at Hailey for approval. She simply raised her head and smiled.

THE WHOLE DRIVE BACK TO OUR HOUSE, I JUST KEPT wondering if this was really happening. I was a little worried that maybe Hailey wasn't okay with coming to our house, but I really wish if that were the case she would grow some balls and speak up. I would definitely put the kibosh on anything I didn't feel comfortable doing. Maybe she was worried we would try to persuade them to ditch their soft-swap rule to go all the way with us. We were totally planning to do that, by the way.

We pulled into the garage and let them in the side door. Maybe not as glamorous as going in the front door and walking through our beautiful, elegant foyer, but hey, these are people who were going to see us naked in a bit. Why not dispense with formalities from the get-go? I asked them if they were ready to try the hot tub, and they both nodded eagerly.

"Great, we have wine down in the basement too, plus beer and hard liquor if you prefer that. Valley is a pretty excellent mixologist if I do say so myself."

"Aw, thanks, honey!" I gushed, squeezing my husband's firm ass cheeks as we led the way down the basement stairs.

"There's a half bath right over there," I pointed to the corner. "It's kind of cramped for more than one person but we can take turns changing if you want. I will grab some towels from the closet over here."

I turned to head toward the closet next to the bath when Hailey's small, perky voice echoed across the vast space of the basement. "I'm fine with changing here," she said, pulling her dress strap down to expose her bare shoulder. "I mean we're going to all see each other naked in a minute anyway, aren't we?"

How could I argue with that logic? I grinned at her and said, "Good point!" I pulled my skirt down around my ankles so that soon I stood in just my strappy stiletto heels, black thong and a flowing beaded camisole with a paisley print. Hailey upped the ante by throwing her dress over the barstool. Once again, no bra. *Hell, if I had firm, perky tits like hers, I wouldn't wear a bra either.*

I slid my camisole over my head and lifted my eyes to see Evan's expression. I could see his eyes had clouded over with lust. He licked his lips as he waited for me to undo the hooks and uncage my full breasts. Soon I was wearing only the black thong and the stilettos, my eyes locked onto Evan's.

"Uh, men, I think it's your turn!" Hailey announced. I was glad she was stepping up. I didn't want to totally run the show here, and thankfully she now seemed on board with moving things forward. I wondered why she had been so demure in the restaurant, but it didn't really matter now…not as long as I was about to see what Evan was working with.

David pulled his black shirt over his head, revealing his fit, sculpted chest. He trimmed his chest hair so it wasn't so thick, but it still offered a nice, manly covering over his tight mounds of pecs and abs. He began to undo his belt buckle and slide his trousers down his legs when he glanced up at Hailey.

She was now 100% nude, having taken off her own leopard print thongs and sky-high platform wedges. She looked so petite standing there, I suddenly realized how fortuitous it was that she was on top in our little 69 session the other night at the party. Otherwise I might have crushed her with my 36 DDs and wide hips.

Now all eyes were on Evan as if to say "Hurry up!" He smirked, his blue eyes flashing as he took his time unbut- toning his navy shirt. He made quite a show of moving his hips and flexing his arms as he began to reveal his body. He was shorter than David, maybe 5'10" and had a thick, weightlifter type of build. *Mmmm...* He was quite the tasty specimen with his broad shoulders, bulging biceps and lots of definition in his thighs.

The way he was strutting around was a relief. I thought at first maybe he was shy. I guess he and Hailey were just holding out on us.

David went on out to the patio to get the hot tub ready while Evan finished his strip tease. Unlike David, he stopped at his tight black boxer briefs. David had walked out to the patio with nothing but a towel wrapped around his waist. I felt a bit deprived. *Take off your boxers, dude!* I wanted to shout. *Reciprocity and all that.* But I guessed I couldn't say much because I was still wearing the black thong. Not that it left much to the imagination!

As sexily as I could, I hooked my thumbs underneath the elastic sides and shimmied my hips as I slid the silky material down my legs. Then I stepped out of them as gracefully as I could, finally removing my heels so I was back to my normal 5'8" height. That was probably a relief to Evan anyway as with the heels on, I was definitely taller than him.

Even though I'm a pretty outspoken person who is 100% genuine at all times and doesn't put up with any level of BS, I'm still the good hostess type, and I absolutely hate it if I sense that anyone feels the slightest bit uncomfortable. That's why I bit my lip and still didn't say a word when Evan didn't take off his boxers. *He'll take them off when we get out there*, I thought to myself. *Surely! We're all completely nude over here!*

The three of us joined David on the patio with the towels still around us. I hesitated for a moment before dropping my towel, using my peripherals to scan the perimeter of my property for nosy neighbors. Fortunately the house next to us was still vacant. And I was pretty sure no one else would have been able to see but the occupants of that house. I turned to our guests and grinned. "Let's go for it!"

The steam rose into the night air, which had actually become somewhat cool for this time of the year. As soon as the breeze hit my nipples, they became impossibly hard, hard enough to cut glass. Or maybe it was the way Evan stared at me with hunger in his eyes. As I was climbing in I noticed him slipping off his boxer briefs and setting them on the patio table.

It's about freaking time! my inner sarcastic bitch shouted, the one who has next to no patience with anyone.

I made myself comfortable in the tub as Hailey joined me, taking the spot right next to me. I glanced up at Evan, and he had moved his hands right over his privates, shielding them from my view. *What the hell was wrong with this man? Was he trying to tease me?* I wanted to see the fucking goods. Oh, what an appropriate use of the word fucking!

David climbed in and took the spot on the other side of me until I shot him a dirty glare, then he realized he needed to move to Hailey's side in order to facilitate some swapping action. This was all a highly calculated, strategic dance, all about positioning oneself so as to reap the highest chances of reward. How could he make out with her if he was clear across the hot tub?

Finally Evan worked his way into the bubbling cauldron of desire, still maintaining the protective shield over his twig and berries. I was afraid at this point it was going to be anticlimactic when I finally got to see them. After all, he hadn't had an erection when he was standing there in his boxer briefs. I would have been able to tell as those puppies don't hide a damn thing!

So, seeing me naked didn't have that type of effect on him... I tried not to dwell on that and instead created a hundred different reasons why he might not have gotten hard at the sight of my naked body: *1. He's thinking about his kids. 2. He's nervous about tonight. 3. He's not sure Hailey is really okay with this. 4. He's wondering if he left the iron on.* You know, standard things.

"It's okay, Evan; I won't bite you," I said, my voice

streaming out like strands of silk. "Not unless you want me to, I mean." I winked suggestively at him, and he finally pulled his hands away as he moved toward the seat next to me. In the light from the hot tub, I got a small glimpse of his tool. *Let's put it this way: I was really hoping he was a grower, not a show-er, if you get my drift. Sigh.*

David's eyes met mine as if to check in with me. I gave him the slightest nod, and he smiled, then turned toward Hailey, stroking his hand down her cheek. "Is it okay to kiss you?" I heard him whisper, obviously not too quietly as it was clear even over the gurgling of the jets.

She nodded and giggled a bit, almost like a schoolgirl instead of a grown woman who has been in the lifestyle for a while. I couldn't figure these two out. They were brash and bold in moments, and demure and reserved in others. *What game are they playing?* I wondered, but before I could contemplate the answers, Evan had rested his hand on my thigh.

I turned toward him as the corners of his lips curled up. "I've been dying to kiss you since that first night at the party," he admitted. "Your lips look like they'd taste incredible."

I couldn't help but return his smile. "Really? Well, there's only one way to find out…" He almost swallowed my last words as his mouth crashed into mine. He pulled me into his strong, muscular arms, and I felt hot water drip down my back from his fingers.

When it cooled in the night air, it sent a surge of electricity through me, along with his tongue as he delved into my mouth to explore. I opened wider to deepen our kiss and heard him moan, and I swear, it was the sexiest sound I've ever heard come out of a man's mouth. I didn't even bother to look over and see what David and Hailey were doing. Oh, no, I was quite happy seeing how this would play out…

Hot tubs are basically a magic elixir, soothing away any inhibitions without the negative side effects of alcohol, like that whole fumbly, slurred-speech kinda thing. The moment I looked over at David and Hailey playing tonsil hockey, his hands fondling her barely-there breasts, I knew we were on the right track. Even after so many years together, I hadn't ever wanted him as much as I wanted him right in that moment.

Most women would slap me upside the head and tell me there's no way they could watch their man with another woman. They'd be too jealous, too worried he'd find something he liked better. But I didn't have any of those thoughts. All I could think of was how hot he looked with another woman's legs wrapped around him, and how she looked in breathless rapture as she realized what an amazing kisser David is. Because I know beyond a shadow of a doubt that David and I are soulmates. It wouldn't matter if a Victoria's Secret model rocked his world, he would always come back to me. It was just the truth of the matter.

He seemed to know I was thinking of him, and I saw his eyes open into a narrow slit until they caught sight of me staring at him. When I saw the grin etch across his face, I knew he felt it too.

So we didn't fuck Evan and Hailey that night. I don't know how long we boiled ourselves in the hot tub, groping, kissing and fondling every available body part, but at some point in time, Hailey came up for air. "Honey?" She tapped her husband on his shoulder to get his attention.

When he looked at her, he knew. They communicated solely with their eyes. It was time to go. I don't know if it was a matter of having to get their kids from the babysitter's or just knowing that they were about to cross the point of no return, but it was time. They thanked us for having them over, said they had a wonderful time, and then made their way out of the hot tub and into the house to change back into their clothes.

They both gave me a kiss on the lips goodbye, and I got one final ass-squeeze of Evan's perfect tushie in before they disappeared into the dark, chilly May night. I turned to David, knowing we had the house to ourselves for the rest of the night, and beckoned him back to the hot tub.

"I just got dressed, Valley!" he protested as I started to rip his clothes off him.

"Shut up and get in so I can ride your cock," I demanded, and to that he had no retort. As soon as his torso was submerged in the bubbling water, I climbed back in, straddling his thighs and maneuvering his thick shaft into my hungry hole. I hadn't been this worked up for a while, and I wasn't doing anything until I let a glorious orgasm relieve the built-up pressure in my core.

"Why do you think they left?" David whispered as I continued to move up and down on him.

I shrugged, words not really available to me at the time. But then I managed: "They're probably going to go home and fuck each other senseless. Kinda like what I'm going to do to you."

I was probably on my fifth orgasm when we realized how pruny our skin was getting. David helped me out of the hot tub, where we dried off and barely made it into the basement before he bent me over the leather loveseat and began to plow into me again. This time his strokes were deep, fast and hard, and with every thrust, my boobs banged into the top ridge of the loveseat. I was probably going to have a bruise against my chest, but I didn't care. It was just as orgasm #6 claimed me that he groaned and released his seed deep inside me.

Later we curled up together in bed, and he asked, "So what do we do now?"

I was transported back to adolescence as I came up with the answer, "I guess we wait for them to call?"

"How was David's work event?" Jenna asked as she opened the door so I could enter.

"Oh…" I took a quick, sharp breath as my mind scrambled to make sense of her question. "Oh! It was great!"

"That was last night, right?" she questioned, an eyebrow raised.

"Yeah, yeah. I'm sorry, I'm just a wee bit hungover," I lied, making the international sign for "tiny" with my thumb and forefinger.

Jenna seemed to think I was flustered about being hungover and not about having had a naked couple in my hot tub the night before, so score one for Valley. Fortunately, I was spared from any further awkwardness by

Aubrey rushing into the kitchen to show me all the crafty things she'd made with Jenna and her girls.

"And I made this one for YOU, Mommy!" she exclaimed, holding out a small, beaded bracelet.

It looked way too tiny to fit on my wrists, and I shot Jenna a worried look.

"Oh, don't worry, the band is elastic!" she assured me, grinning.

I smiled as I carefully stretched the pink and purple beads over my hand and slid them down onto my wrist. "How pretty! Did you have fun?"

"Yes!" She jumped up and down with excitement. "I wanna come back next week!"

"She's such a good girl. She's welcome anytime!"

Oh, good, I sighed with relief. I had a feeling Mr. and Mrs. Archer would be needing overnight sitters a great deal in the immediate future…

8

Our inbox was full. I couldn't believe how much mail we were sorting through every night. Then I realized why: the site had a testimonial feature. So, basically, other users could leave a little blurb verifying we were real people and whether or not we were any fun. We had received a couple of them now and being legit meant more people were making a move on us.

I say "real people" because Ed and Shawna had warned us about single men masquerading as a couple. But there were even more nefarious infractions ranging from people who used severely outdated photos so that when they met other lifestyle folks in person, they were hardly recognizable to one horror story Ed and Shawna told us about a couple from one of these sites who stole the identities of another couple.

I guess when they had just finished doing the deed in a hotel room, and the one couple went to shower and clean up, the con artists stole their wallets and high-tailed it out of there. That's some scary shit right there. David's eyes looked roughly the size of planets when they were filling us in on that little tidbit.

Ed and Shawna left us a testimonial that read, "D & V are a super sweet, sexy couple we had the pleasure of getting to know over dinner a few weeks ago. Definitely do not pass up an opportunity to meet these two! They're the whole package."

"Aww, isn't that sweet?" I asked David as I read it out loud to him. "Oh, and there's a new one from Evan and Hailey."

David's ears immediately perked. See, I knew he liked Hailey a lot more than he had been letting on. Every day since the night in the hot tub he asked me if they had contacted us. I didn't get much feedback from them other than a text the following morning that read, "Had a great time! Hope to see you again soon!"

I don't know if we were expecting a report card or what. *David and Valley get an A for hospitality, a B+ for kissing and an A+ for oral skills. Haha!*

Their testimonial was similarly brief. "We met V & D recently at a party and then hung out in their hot tub a couple of weeks later. They are attractive, conversational, and did we mention they have a hot tub? What's not to like?!"

"So that's okay, right?" David questioned.

I nodded. "I think so. It's not like they said anything bad. We should probably leave one for them too."

"So I guess we are D and V," he noted, chuckling. "Well, I guess it would be indiscreet to give out people's names, even if they are only first names."

"Not only that, but I'm probably the only 'Valley' on the entire site!"

"No doubt! So what should we say about E & H?"

My fingers floated over the keys as I tried to concoct something complimentary yet witty. "Okay, how about this?" I asked, beginning to type and read as I went. "E & H are a hot, sexy couple we hope to see a lot more of in the future. They are welcome in our hot tub any time!"

"Short, sweet, and to the point," David assessed. "I think that will work."

I pressed enter, and then a little green check appeared on their profile to indicate a new testimonial. I quickly glanced through the rest of the testimonials they had—five in total—and saw they all said basically the same thing as mine. *So much for originality!* As I was reading, we heard a ding announcing a new email.

"Oh, we are extremely popular tonight!" David laughed as I hovered over the mail icon with the mouse cursor.

"Oh!" I gasped as I read it. I wasn't sure whether to be flattered or freaked out. "Hey, you two—we just saw your profile and recognize you from the party Ed and Shawna threw a few weeks ago. We're hosting a meet and greet at The Bay Club on Saturday and wondered if you might want to come? Let us know! Kisses, Joel and Katie."

"They recognized us from our naked torsos?" David asked, almost as flabbergasted as I was by the notion. "I mean your boobs are pretty epic, but—"

"Oh, I bet it's from the testimonials," I finally realized, breathing a sigh of relief. *Though several people did see me naked when Hailey and I were playing in one of the bedrooms. Maybe my boobs had a cult following now?*

"Ohhhhh," David grinned. "Yeah, that makes more

sense. But Saturday? After we just got sitters last week. I don't know, honey; what do you think?"

I let out a sigh as I did some mental calculations. I didn't want to ruin my neighborly goodwill with Jenna and Posey by asking them to keep Aidan and Aubrey again overnight. Then I remembered our other secret weapon: my in-laws. They hadn't seen the kids in a while, so they were due for a visit. Now what story could I concoct to get them to stay overnight?

EVERY TIME MY MOTHER-IN-LAW SHOWS UP WITH THAT snide look on her face, I want to slap it right off her. The original Mrs. Archer is a tall, elegant lady who looks like she raided Katharine Hepburn's closet. Basically, her style is at the conservative end of the spectrum, while mine is on an entirely different spectrum. She always gave me a reproachful once-over when I greeted her at the door, and tonight was no different.

We'd come up with quite a story for our overnight getaway. My college roommate was getting married in a small, private ceremony a few towns over, so David and I were getting a hotel room and staying the night.

"So you mean you intend to get drunk?" Joanna Archer had asked in her deep, stern voice when David explained it to her over the phone, which was on speaker, so I had the pleasure of hearing the thick stench of disapproval echo into the room.

"Drunk and laid!" I shouted from the other side of the bed. David had clasped his hand over his iPhone and shot me a death glare.

So I wore a dress I thought would convey semi-appropriate wedding attire. It was a black and white print strapless number with an A-line skirt, so it didn't even cling to my hips. And she still gave me a look as though my shoulders were crafted by Satan himself. I slipped on a black shrug, and her expression changed to one of barely-contained glee.

"Aubrey, Aidan, your grandparents are here!" I called up the stairs, hoping the kids wouldn't dilly dally so David and I could get on our way. We really had gotten a hotel room at The Bay Club, and I planned to get ready for the real party there. That's right, the somewhat demure dress was only a decoy. *Bwahahahahaha!*

I was also hoping for some pre-game action, if you get my drift. *wink* Poor David, little did he know I planned to have my way with him before I turned him loose on the other women at the party.

I heard the kids' footsteps thundering down the wooden staircase. Who knows how two individuals who together probably still weigh less than I do can make 3x as much noise with their feet? I didn't have time to think too seriously about yet another universal paradox when there were boobs to be squeezed and dicks to be licked. I kissed my spawn goodbye, gave my in-laws each a quick pat on the back of gratitude, and we were on our way.

THE BAY CLUB WAS ON THE NORTH SIDE OF SUNVIEW. IT only took us about twenty minutes to get there, and that was with somewhat heavy traffic. We checked in, got our freak on (David balked at the idea of expending too much energy before the party, so I did most of the work myself), and then I spent some time bathing and ladyscaping before the main attraction.

I was feeling rather on top of my A Game by the time I emerged from the bathroom wearing a skin-tight curve-hugging silver sequined dress and an absolutely fabulous pair of hot pink stilettos. I probably wouldn't have believed them myself if I hadn't seen them call to me from the store window. I swear those heels made my panties wet, they were so damn hot!

"You ready to go?" David asked from the bed, where he had been half-ass watching baseball and playing some juvenile game Aidan got him addicted to on his phone.

"Do I look ready to you?" I asked a little more sarcastically than I intended, especially since he barely looked up from his game to acknowledge me. I was hoping for a bit more of a reaction to my ensemble than a nonchalant grunt.

He shoved his phone back in his pocket and rolled off the bed. As soon as he stood upright and turned to look at me, I witnessed his face carving into a wide grin as his eyes traveled from my head to my feet and back again. "Wow, baby...you look amazing!"

"It's about damn time you noticed!" I teased him, stepping toward him. He pulled me into his arms and planted his lips on mine. I broke our kiss and pulled him toward the door.

"What's the hurry?" he asked, his eyes traveling back down to my spectacular décolletage.

"Oh, no, you already had your chance at this. It's someone else's turn now!" I laughed as I grabbed my sparkly clutch purse off the bureau, then ushered him out the door.

My stilettos pushed into the plush carpeting all the way to the elevator. When the doors opened, we joined another couple, who was also going down to the lobby level. When the man turned to look at me, I bit my lower lip and squeezed David's hand. Then I immediately wished I hadn't because, of course, he looked up at me and asked, "What?" thereby gaining the attention of the male half of the couple.

"Well, if it isn't David Archer!" the man exclaimed in a boisterous baritone, slapping my husband on the back.

"Oh, hello there, Bob," David answered, his eyes shooting down to me as if to ask me to cover up my body. I am not sure how I was supposed to do that, but the request was clearly conveyed. I wrapped my arms around my chest, but I think it only made my cleavage more apparent. I could tell Bob's wife was less than impressed.

Bob Clark was on the board of the Catholic church that David was in the process of rendering a design for their new building. I cringed thinking of what he and his wife Barbara, at least twenty years our senior, were doing at The Bay Club. If they were there for the same party we were, I was probably going to melt into a pile of mortified goo all over the elevator floor at any moment. Some unlucky bastard was going to have to come and scrape me off. Hopefully at least my beautiful shoes would come through unscathed.

There was silence for the next three floors until the elevator landed with a thud at the lobby level. It dinged as it opened, and Bob and his wife waited for David and me to exit. I was hoping they were going to proceed through the lobby toward the exit, but no, of course not. They followed us into the grand hallway where the ballrooms were located. There were two ballrooms on each side, one was the Starfish Ballroom, and the other was the Sand Dollar Ballroom. The four of us stood awkwardly under the exquisite crystal chandelier, trying to figure out which direction we were supposed to go.

"Are you here for the Catholic League Awards Banquet too?" Bob asked with a grin. "I'm getting the Lifetime Achievement award tonight!"

"Oh, that's wonderful!" I patted him on the back and turned to Barbara. "You must be so proud! David, I need to use the restroom, so I'll meet you in the room in a few minutes, alright?" I touched my husband's arm and gave him a look that said *follow my lead*.

"I should really make a pit stop first too. Maybe we're at the same table, Bob! See you in a few." He bent down to give Barbara a quick peck on the cheek, then shook Bob's hand before following me toward the restrooms at the far end of the hall.

Once we were out of earshot, I glanced over to make sure they'd gone inside before I burst into hysterical laughter. I was laughing so hard, I worried that my mascara might get ruined.

"Why are you laughing?" David grasped my elbow and jerked me upright. "That wasn't funny at all!"

"Oh, come on! It was hilarious!" I argued.

"What if they find out we aren't here for the Catholic League awards and instead are here for a swinger party?"

I shook my head, swallowing the rest of the giggles that were trying to bubble up my throat. I pulled him over to the ballroom on the other side of the room. The sign outside read "Grayson-Marks Reception." I pointed to it with pursed lips as if to say *I told you so.*

But I didn't have to say any words at all. He sighed with relief and ushered me through the doors. I'm sorry, but the fact the swinger party was happening across the hall from the Catholic awards banquet could not go without a laugh. *That's some funny shit right there!*

THE VIBE AT THE MEET AND GREET SEEMED A LOT different than the house party we'd attended at Ed and Shawna's. It was more formal, like a wedding reception or a prom—only if it were produced by the same fine folks who brought us *Girls Gone Wild* back in the 90s. The ladies were wearing slinky summer dresses and heels to die for. It turned out my fuchsia stilettos weren't the hottest heels on the block, though definitely top five.

Instead of having the decorum of a wedding reception (at least before everyone gets hammered), this party featured random acts of drunkenness from the get-go, accompanied by the occasional flash of titties and heavy make-out sessions on the dance floor, often between two women.

I was mesmerized by all the beautiful people. It was like a sexual smorgasbord, where you could walk around and decide which treats you might want to sample later or which dishes might make the best entrees. Some of the gentlemen looked as though they could provide a full meal, if you get my drift.

We found Joel and Katie over by the DJ as they were handing him some suggestions for music to play. It wasn't long after their chat that the music turned less Top-40 and more what we probably listened to in high school and college. That meant a serious throwback to the 80s and 90s. *Not that I'm complaining. It's loads better than the shit that passes for music now.*

Joel greeted me with a kiss right smack dab on the lips, and I immediately tasted a tinge of rum on his mouth. It made me want to take him aside and see what other flavors I could sample. Katie was all over David as if she had similar notions, and I had a fleeting thought that perhaps tonight's hosts would end up becoming our first full swap.

Speaking of which, I was pretty sure Evan and Hailey were not going to be in attendance due to babysitting issues, but then I saw them on the dance floor with another couple. He was a handsome Black man, who looked tall enough to be a pro basketball player. The woman was a curvy Latina with tight, curly hair that sprang out all around her beautiful face. *So I guess Evan wasn't lying when he said he loved curves.*

I shrugged that off. It's not like they didn't know we were coming. David even flashed me a look when he noticed them, and I just rolled my eyes and continued to look around the room. It was a split second later that some woman came up to David and asked if he wanted to dance.

He looked at me as if to ask permission, and I simply nodded. *So this lady wants my man? I can dig it.* I looked around the space to see if I could spot her man so we could get some reciprocal action up in here.

I didn't see where she had come from, but the next thing I knew, Katie was asking me if I would help her with something in the bathroom. I shrugged as I glanced at Joel, who just wore an evil smirk on his face, so I thought maybe there was some sort of secret code I didn't know about. I followed Katie into the ladies' room, and she pulled me into one of the stalls. *What the actual fuck was going on here?*

"Uh, what's up?" I questioned, feeling some creepy vibes travel up my spine. It felt a little strange to be confronted in a tiny bathroom stall. Okay, it was the handicapped stall, so it wasn't tiny. There was space and all, but it still seemed ultra-weird to me. I didn't even really know this chick.

"Sorry to ambush you like this, but I need to know something," she said, searching my face with her dark eyes.

"Okay?" I was having a hard time shaking the weird feeling I had.

"We saw you talking to those people out in the hallway before you came into the party tonight." Before she could even get the whole sentence out, her cheeks reddened, and her eyes filled with tears.

I had to rack my brain to even understand what she was talking about. "Oh, you mean Barbara and Bob?"

"Yes," she breathed out, looking as though she might hyperventilate at any given moment.

"What the hell is wrong with you?" I reached out to touch her shoulder.

"Those are my parents," she sighed, her brows furrowed and tears glistening in the corners of her eyes.

"Whoa, what?" I gasped. "Your parents?"

She looked so shaky all of the sudden, I was afraid she was going to pass out on me. "Yeah. Fuck, I thought my cover was blown. They think we're with my in-laws tonight. What the hell are they doing here, and how do you know them?"

"Okay, take a deep breath, sweetie," I said, putting my arm around her waist and drawing her closer to me. "Just breathe, okay?"

I wanted to make sure she was going to be all right before I answered her questions. The last thing I wanted to happen was for the poor thing collapse on the bathroom floor—then her cover would really get blown. Imagine an ambulance pulling up to the hotel and paramedics running through the lobby with a stretcher for her, all while curious onlookers gaped. And two of those curious onlookers might be her parents.

"We thought our cover was blown too when we saw them!" I laughed. "They are associates of my husband's. He's building the new Catholic church just outside of town. Your dad is in the Catholic League and on the church board, yes?"

She vigorously nodded. "Yes, and they have no idea that Joel and I are swingers!" She whispered the last word with such a violent hiss that it actually came out louder than her other words. *Oops.* I hoped her mom didn't wander into the bathroom while we were talking, though I was pretty sure the bathroom we were using was on the opposite side of the hallway between the two ballrooms. So, hopefully we weren't going to run into anyone who wasn't part of our gathering.

"It's okay, Katie. It's going to be okay. I won't spoil your secret, okay?" I rubbed her back a little, hoping I could calm her down. I wasn't sure what she would be like in bed if she was so flighty in this situation. It now appeared less and less likely that I was going to find out.

"Let's just get you back inside the party," I suggested after she failed to respond to my promise. "I'm sure everything will be fine. Your parents will be out of here long before this party is over."

She took a deep, cleansing breath and tried to wipe the look of worry off her face. "Okay, okay. You're right. Thank you so much. Okay, let's go back inside."

So, for the second time that night, crisis was narrowly averted. I followed Katie back into the ballroom and scanned the premises for my husband. I found him in a dark corner making out with the lady who had asked him to dance. I rolled my eyes.

Okay, okay, that's fine; he's got himself a little admirer.

It was my turn. I started to wonder about our rules for same room play. If it was this hard to hook a couple, were we ever going to be able to get this same room thing to work out?

I headed for the bar. I felt like the answer could only be found at the bottom of a margarita or two.

TWO HOURS LATER, MY HUSBAND HAD BEEN PROPOSITIONED by approximately three and a half women. I say half because the last one was so drunk, she could barely stand, let alone speak. I think she probably would have passed out by the time David got her upstairs to the room, though I was perfectly happy to indulge him in a threesome if he could seal the deal with any of these little hornettes. The problem was once he revealed I would be a part of the mix, they all seemed to turn their nose up.

David told me it was because I was too hot, and they were intimidated by me. *Ha, as if!* Okay, okay, he might have been right about that. Only one of them was really cute. She was petite and wearing a lovely curve-hugging green dress. She had a head full of auburn curls that bounced when she moved on her sexy t-strap heels. She was there with a partner, but he seemed to be interested in a blonde across the room.

She explained they preferred separate room play. "We can just never agree on a couple," she admitted. Then she leaned in to whisper in my ear, "He only likes blondes."

I had to roll my eyes at that remark, and I may have even done the "Whatever" toss-my-jet-black-hair-over-my-shoulder maneuver as well. So I wasn't his type. He looked kind of like a douchebag anyway. "What's your name?" I asked her.

"Caroline," she answered with a flirty bat of her eyelashes. *Great, I would just remember not to invite Caroline and her douchey brunette-hating husband to our first party in our new swinger paradise when it was finished.*

Thirty or forty minutes after the drunk lady hit on David, we decided it was time to retire to our room. Even with our pre-game action, I was raring to go. David looked at me with a bit of surprise painted on his face, "Again?" he questioned.

"Uh, yes, again," I answered. "We were both supposed to get laid tonight after the party, you know!"

"Yes, but we did it before the party," he reminded me for the second time.

"If we had another chick up here, would you fuck

her?" I pinned my eyes to his as I awaited his truthful response.

He swallowed hard, knowing that my lie detector equipment was at least as sensitive as what they use in policework. "Okay, yeah, I would."

"So, what, I'm not good enough for you? Not sexy enough?" I pressed. "Just pretend I'm some other chick if you have to." I began to unzip my dress. "Either way, I need some cock."

"Are you going to pretend I'm some other dude?" he asked with a smirk.

"Hey, whatever it takes," I answered. As soon as my dress was off, I tackled him onto the bed. I unzipped his dress pants and brought out his manhood, which sprang to life under my touch. "Some other chick isn't going to fuck you as well as I will anyway," I argued, staring deeply into his eyes.

"I have no doubt about that," he answered. "No doubt at all."

9

One month into our adventure, and no one has popped our cherry.

Let that sink in for a moment. Here we are, one ridiculously sexy man and one unashamedly curvy MILF, and we cannot seem to get laid to save our lives. We haven't heard from Evan and Hailey or Joel and Katie, for that matter. Heck, we are kind of kicking ourselves for not getting down and dirty with Ed and Shawna when we had the chance, but now they've gone out west to await the birth of their next grandchild and might be gone the rest of the summer.

The website has been an endless circle of frustration. We receive a first message or send one. Pictures are exchanged. Schedules are discussed. But then nothing happens. NOTHING HAPPENS! And we haven't gotten invited to any more parties after the meet and greet at the hotel.

Except that lo and behold I finally got a message back from *AllAboutHer*...a.k.a. Derek...the gorgeous man who travels here on business once a month or so. It turned out he was in town. Now I needed to convince David that I should meet him for a drink.

"So, what do you want to do, go meet him for a drink and then bring him back here to fuck you or what?" David asked, barely looking over his phone at me.

"Uh, I don't know. Why, do you want to go out for a drink with us?" I couldn't hide the flinty sarcasm in my voice.

"I'm sorry, I'm not exactly sure what the protocol is for letting some other dude fuck my wife," David answered, putting his phone on the table next to him, then snapping his eyes to mine.

He hardly ever raises his voice, so to hear him do so took me aback. I made sure the kids were happily engaged downstairs with the Xbox and walked over to him. I may have been swinging my hips, and I might have just nonchalantly flipped my hair over my shoulder as I sashayed in his general direction. When I got close to him, I stopped right between his legs as he sat on the sofa. Then I firmly planted a knee on each side of him and settled my voluptuous ass right down on his thighs.

"What, honey?" he asked, staring into my eyes. I was close enough to him to see the little flecks of gold and amber in his hazel irises. Damn, he just had the sexiest eyes. If the kids weren't right out in the living room, I'd have hiked up my skirt, whipped his cock out and gone to town right there in his office.

"You are so fucking hot," I whispered in my deepest, sultriest voice, leaning down to kiss his neck and then the scruff along his jawline. "Wanna go fuck?"

Normally at this point, I would be able to feel his cock

stiffen against my pussy as I pressed myself against him. But there was nothing. *Nada. Zilch happening in the erection department.* "What's wrong?" I questioned, searching his face for answers I was afraid his voice wouldn't give.

"Nothing is wrong. Didn't we have sex this morning?" he asked. "I am pretty sure you made me late for work and almost made the kids late for school."

I bounced up and down on him with a little pout pushing the corners of my lips down. "I can't help it, David. I'm fucking horny all the time! That's why I was asking about Derek. That's why I want to meet him. We've been trying to get laid for a month now, and it hasn't happened. We haven't even gotten that close except me being with Hailey. And I got into this whole thing because I wanted COCK!"

He shook his head and rolled his eyes at the same time. "You're just insatiable, aren't you?" He ran his fingers through my hair, then trailed them over to my chin, where he angled my face down toward his as though he were going to kiss me.

"Please don't patronize me, okay?" I sat back down and crossed my arms over my chest. "I'm trying to be patient, but patience isn't exactly my thing—"

"Really?" he scoffed. "You don't say!" He chuckled as he wrapped his arms around me and gave me a squeeze.

"Don't you want a guy to come fuck me and give you a night off?" I asked him, sincerely this time.

"Now that you mention it, a night off might be nice." He smiled and this time took my face into both of his hands as he pressed his lips against mine softly. "Valley, I love you; you know that. If this is what you want, we'll make it happen."

"So you think I should go meet him, then?"

"When does he want to meet?"

"Uh, tonight…?"

"So what happens if you want to fuck? You can't bring him back here—the kids are here! It's a school night."

I tapped my feet impatiently against the floor as I waited for a stroke of brilliance to overtake me. "So I'll ask him if he can get together this weekend. Or tomorrow at lunch…the kids will be at school. Could you come home for an hour or two?"

"Just go meet him and see if you even like him first, okay?"

A grin spread across my face. "Okay, honey." I glanced down at my watch. "I'm meeting him in an hour. Better go get ready."

I TRIED TO PULL THE SKIRT OF MY DRESS DOWN A LITTLE further so the enormity of my thighs wasn't hanging out as I made my way into the quaint Irish pub where I was meeting Derek. My heart was pounding. Meeting David in class when we were in college meant I never dated as a grown-up. I mean, sure, I "dated" in high school, like going to the movies with a boy or a school dance. But I've never had the experience of meeting a stranger for the first time at a bar.

I'm normally a pretty secure person. I hardly ever feel embarrassed or shy, but even I was feeling a little out of my element as I chose a barstool and hoisted myself onto it, my eyes anxiously darting around to see if I recognized Derek among the pub patrons. I am thrilled to report that while I was waiting (I arrived a bit early), I did have at least two other men checking me out and a third offered to buy me a drink. *I'm going to chalk that up as a win right there.*

Finally, at about five minutes past our agreed-upon meeting time, the heavy wooden door to the pub swung open and in walked Derek. Okay, so he was a bit shorter than I expected. Why did I think his profile said he was 6 feet? He couldn't have been an inch over 5'8", which is what I am flat-footed. But I didn't care because he had massively broad shoulders and was wearing a fitted V-neck shirt that barely contained his impressive biceps.

David is muscular, but a bit on the wiry side, more like a runner than a bodybuilder. But Derek was…well, he was fucking built. I had to consciously strive to keep the drool from running down my chin when he flashed his gorgeous smile at me.

"Valley?" he confirmed as he made his way toward me. I stood to greet him, feeling a little zing of exhilaration bolt through me.

I went to shake his hand, feeling a bit fumbly, but he pulled me into his arms and squeezed me tightly against his rippled chest. *Holy shit, he is strong!* A vision of him throwing me down on the bed and having his way with me auto-played in my mind.

He took the seat next to me and asked if I'd ordered a drink yet. I shook my head no, so he asked, "What's your poison?" in a voice so deep and sexy, it sent a shiver down my spine.

Once the bartender took our order, I swiveled in my chair to face him, crossing one leg over the other so my dress rode up high on my thigh.

"Damn!" His eyes traveled down my body as my flash of skin captured his attention. "Your pictures don't do you justice, Valley. Not at all."

"I could say the same for you." I gave him another once-over as my lips curled up into a smile. "So you said you travel out this way for business. What kind of business do you do?"

"Sales," he replied quickly. Almost too quickly. It was a pretty vague answer, and the way I just stared at him, waiting for him to elaborate, made him shift a bit on his barstool before continuing, "Medical equipment. I'm the regional sales director for a medical supply company."

"Oh," I said. "Okay. So like...what kind of equipment?"

He looked a bit mortified that I was probing into his professional life. I guess these types of meetings were really just all about sex? So sue me for wanting to get to know a little bit about the guy who was going to stick his dick in me.

Oh, so I guess I decided I wanted him to stick his dick in me? That's why we're meeting, right? I regrouped when I saw his expression gave away that he was a bit put-off by my questioning. "Sorry, you don't have to answer that. I guess we're supposed to—"

"No, it's okay. I sell surgical products mostly. It's not that big of a deal. Just a job." He gave me the sexiest little shrug I've ever seen as his eyes flashed down and then back up again to meet mine head on.

"So you're not married...or...anything?" I glanced down at his left hand to check if there was a ring, or a tan line where a ring had been. *Negative.*

"I'm divorced. No kids. I travel a lot—it's hard on a marriage." His eyes fluttered down to my breasts, which were perfectly poised in my black lace push-up bra. I saw an appreciative smile creep across his face before his eyes met mine again. *I think that look could be what some refer to as eye-fucking.*

"I bet. I can't imagine that would be easy on anyone." I wondered if he got the sense that I was eye-fucking him right back?

"Right. What about you and the Mister?"

"He's an architect. I'm an interior designer," I answered almost as quickly as he had blurted out he was in sales.

"Oh, now that sounds like a match made in heaven!" His blue-green eyes sparkled as the bartender finally brought us our drinks. He took a healthy sip of his scotch after clinking his glass with my martini.

"It was when we were first married. We worked on a lot of projects together. But now I stay home with our kids and write an interior design blog," I explained. *Yikes. I can't think of anything less sexy than the words that just came out of my mouth. Fuck me. No, really. Fuck me. Can I just say that? Can we just skip ahead now to the fucking?*

"And post sexy pictures of yourself on swinger websites?" he queried, his eyes piercing mine. In his mind, I am pretty sure I was already half-undressed. He looked like he wanted to eat me alive, and he'd get no complaints from me on that front. We were definitely kicking up some serious pheromones in here. If there were a pheromone detector, it would be going fucking crazy right about now.

"I have been meaning to take some new ones, actually. Possibly some…uh…action shots…" I may or may not have suggestively licked my bottom lip after saying that. *Okay, I did. I totally did.*

"I wouldn't mind being part of that photo shoot. Maybe I could serve as a prop or something..." He laughed and mimicked my lip-lick with his own. *Holy mother of fuck!*

It didn't take me long to guzzle down my drink. After all, I needed it to quench the fire that was building between my legs. Unfortunately, the buzz that came over me from finishing my drink so quickly only seemed to intensify the burn.

"So what else do I need to know about you, Derek?" I questioned, my voice managing to come out smooth as spun silk.

"My username? It's pretty accurate." He grinned broadly enough for me to see his straight, white teeth. "Meaning anything that gets you off...will get me off."

Damn. AllAboutHer, I reminded myself of his swinger site alter ego. My mind was already racing off with the possibilities. I didn't even know where to start. "So, like oral? You like giving oral?"

David didn't mind going down on me every once in a while, but he always complained that he needed a snorkel and mask to do a proper job.

"I love giving oral." Derek licked his lips again as if to prove the veracity of his statement. "Love it. The wetter the better."

"I think we're going to get along very well," I assured him. "Very well."

"So when can we find out?" he pressed. "Would you like to come back to my room?"

Oh, god. The word "yes" was just dangling on my tongue, waiting to be used, but then the angel on my shoulder popped an image of David into my head, patiently waiting for me at home.

"I would love to," I said, trying to fight off the angel, whose wings were flapping furiously as she stomped up and down on my neck. "But, as I said in my email, we're a package deal."

He smiled and nodded with understanding. "I know. But a guy's gotta try, right?"

I couldn't help but be flattered. "Of course. I don't know if my husband will just want to watch or take part. We're pretty new at this."

"Oh, really? You don't seem...uninitiated to me," he observed. "You come across as pretty experienced, the type of woman who knows what she wants and just goes for it."

I let a tiny laugh escape past my lips, slipping past the "yes" that was still waiting to be used. "Well, I *do* know what I want...and I *do* want to go for it...but I have to follow the rules."

"Of course," he agreed. "So, when can we make this happen?"

"Do you have any availability during the day?" I asked with hope dripping off my words.

A few minutes later, we were making arrangements for him to visit after lunch the next day. We'd have two hours before the kids needed to be picked up from school. Thank god for David having a flexible work schedule.

We both ordered another drink, and I got to know a little more about Derek, including his obsessions with craft beer, 90s grunge bands, and kitesurfing. He was an interesting mix of boyish and masculine, and I couldn't wait to see how those two sides of him interacted in the bedroom.

After another hour of flowing conversation, he walked me to my car. The night air was just beginning to thin, and the humidity had lost its oppressiveness with the gentle breeze blowing in from the west. There were parts of me that wanted to throw him in the back seat of my car and have all of my curiosities satisfied...not to mention my rampant horniness. But I kept telling myself that good things come to those who wait. *That's what they say, right?*

He stood for a moment, his eyes crawling tentatively over my face as if he were trying to decide his next move. He wrapped his arms around my waist and gave me a gentle hug before whispering in my ear, "Would it be okay if I kissed you?"

His words sent a shiver shuddering through me. I pulled back far enough to lock my gaze with his, and even in the moonlight I could see the desire flickering in his eyes. I wanted so much more than a kiss, but it would be a start. I didn't even answer, I just took his face into my palms and softly brushed my lips against his, waiting for him to decide the next move.

His muscular arms enveloped me, pulling me closer to him as he deepened our kiss, tasting me with his tongue as his musky scent filled my nostrils. He smelled positively scrumptious, and my pussy began to respond to him even though I had tried to keep her under control. I have a feeling if she had her way, we'd both be stripping down and getting it on right there on the hood of my car in the parking lot.

Good thing she's down there and her lips can't speak, and I'm up here in command.

"I can't wait to see you tomorrow, Valley," he said as though he just wanted to hear my name on his lips one more time before we parted company. Then he walked off to his car, leaving me staggering in the moonlight, trying to recapture my breath.

"ARE YOU SURE YOU SAID ONE O'CLOCK?" DAVID questioned, his eyes scanning my face with a hint of desperation, of helplessness.

He is such a dear. He really, really hates disappointing me. He hates disappointing me so much that he's beside himself even when someone else is responsible for disappointing me.

I'd checked my texts at least ten times and the swinger website too. No messages from Derek. No indication at all that he was or wasn't showing up, but by the looks of my empty driveway, it looks like he was a no-show.

Where the hell was he?

I had no fucking clue. I couldn't believe after the chemistry between us the night before that he would just ghost me like this. I came home from our date, told David how promising it was, and tried my hardest not to gush too gratuitously about what a great kisser Derek was, how sexy his voice was, or how hot his bulging biceps were. I played it cool, of course. David seemed genuinely excited for me.

And now here we were at one-thirty in the afternoon —and there was no sign of Derek.

David paced across the basement, which we'd started to transform into my dream swinger party space. But I was so angry, I felt like punching a hole in the new drywall where the bathroom was going to be.

If I had a baseball bat, I might take it to the glass doors that led to the patio. Just looking at that hot tub made me angry because it was a symbol of our whole swinger mojo that seemed to be going down the drain. Why didn't anyone want to fuck me? *I mean us...*

David knew I was pissed because I got quiet. *A quiet Valley is an angry Valley—and is not to be messed with.* Nevertheless he walked straight over to me, took my face into his hands and began to kiss me, with tongue and all. Then he began to unbuckle the belt holding up his black dress pants. Clearly he planned to take matters into his own hands.

I broke away. "What are you doing?"

"What does it look like I'm doing?" he questioned, his brows furrowing and his lips pursed. "I'm going to fuck my wife. You're horny, right?"

I shook my head. "No, no. That's not that I want you to do. I don't want you to just pacify me with your cock. I'm genuinely upset here."

I hated to admit it, but he almost looked relieved. And that made me even more mad because it was apparent he didn't even want to have sex with me. He *was* just trying to pacify me with his cock. *Damn it!* I let out a giant huff of exasperation and stormed out the patio doors. Of course, I couldn't be dramatic and slam them because they're almost all glass, and even as much as I felt like shattering them to pieces, I knew I needed to put on my big girl panties and get ahold of myself.

I'd been like this since I was a child. My mother would tell you I'm a spoiled brat because I tend to throw a fit when I don't get my way. The last time I remember throwing a fit of epic proportions was when my daughter was breech, and they thought they were going to have to take her by C-section.

I absolutely refused to have a scar marring my bikini line, so I read every fucking piece of info I could get on turning a breech baby, and then I put that fucking plan into action. David called it Project Somersault because that's essentially what we were trying to get Aubrey to do. But you should have seen the stink I raised in my OB's office when she wouldn't even try to do an ECV—the procedure to turn a breech baby. I had to take matters into my own hands.

I had to take matters into my own hands then, and maybe I needed to take them into my hands once more. I stormed down the sidewalk around the hot tub and across the yard, then around the side of the house toward the front. We live on a cul-de-sac with seven houses, at the end of a quiet street called Juniper Court. I knew we had at least two neighbors who were single men. I wondered if either of them would be up for a threesome.

The newest neighbor had just moved in a few days ago, and I probably should have done the neighborly thing of showing up with a welcome basket and some fresh-baked cookies, but I think I was too busy trying to get laid. *So could I show up now and offer him a freshly shaved pussy? Wouldn't that be better anyway?* He looked cute from what I could tell when he was moving stuff in.

Then there was the guy across the street, Greer. I always saw him outside mowing without a shirt on, and he never seemed to pay me one bit of attention. But then I saw him outside with a little girl and realized he is a single dad. *That's just so fucking adorable, it only makes him hotter.*

I wondered if I just went up to him and cut to the chase, if he would come over for a dip in the hot tub. Maybe Jenna could watch his kid too? I wondered if I should just cut to the chase with Jenna too, tell her the whole story and enlist her help to make sure I finally get my threesome.

I got into this whole swinging business for a three-some, and I couldn't even make it happen. I felt like an utter failure. What good did it do me to have three dozen men send me messages saying "ur so sexy," if I couldn't actually get one of them to show up when he said he would?

After taking a quick walk around the cul de sac, I real-ized that neither the new neighbor, Erik, or the one across the street, Greer, were home. I guess they had jobs and stuff. But I was serious about striking up a friendship with them.

How convenient would that be? Maybe I could just sneak one of them into the house at night. Once we got our basement done, it would be virtually sealed off from the rest of the house—David and I could do just about anything down there, and no one would be the wiser...

I made my way home and spotted David sitting on the porch waiting for me. His eyes still looked kind and sympathetic. But I didn't want sympathy. I wanted to be fucked. To be taken. I wanted Derek to prove his user-name *AllAboutHer* to be true. And now I just had a serious case of blue balls...er...ovaries.

"Come here," David said as I climbed up the steps and onto the porch. I didn't want to, but I did.

I fell into his arms where he held me tightly against his chest. "We just got started, honey. It will work out eventually; I promise. That guy was clearly a douche, and he is definitely missing out on the best pussy on the planet. Prime, grade A, platinum pussy," David assured me.

I wrapped my arms around him and squeezed him back. I knew I was selfish for wanting more than I had right there in my arms. I felt bad about that. I was just hoping for a different outcome. I reached up to give David a kiss on the edge of his lips, but he took my face into his palms again and kissed me deeply, stirring something inside of me I thought was too angry to come out.

Within seconds, our kiss heated up to such a level that we needed to go inside before any neighbors who were home (*I'm looking at YOU, Mr. Sullivan*) got a show...

10

When I stepped outside to get our mail, I was surprised to see our neighbor Nina heading toward me with a thick envelope in her hand. She had a neutral expression on her face, so I had no idea what she was about to lay on me, but I really hoped we hadn't inadvertently pissed off the homeowners' association with the construction noise coming from our basement project.

"Hi, Nina, what's up?" I greeted her with a warm smile on my face. I also hoped she hadn't noticed her husband's apparent fascination with me. That certainly wouldn't be well-received.

"Hey, this was in my mailbox, but I think it belongs to you and David?" She shot me a questioning glance as she pushed the envelope out toward me.

My eyebrows quirked as I turned it over and saw the logo stamped in the return address area: *Desire Resorts*. As soon as it registered, my heart began to thunder against my ribcage.

"Everything okay?" she asked, her eyebrows flying up to the same heights mine had already achieved.

I tried to resist the urge to break out my best dance moves; it was so hard to contain my excitement! I had booked a week at an all-inclusive lifestyle resort for our anniversary, which was coming up in October, and I was waiting for the packet of information to arrive so I could surprise David.

"Oh my god, thank you SO much for bringing this over!" I squeezed the envelope to my chest as I began to imagine all the fun we were going to have on the white sand beaches of this beautiful swinger paradise.

"Yeah, no problem," Nina answered, but her curiosity was obviously not satisfied. "So, uh, what is it?"

"I booked a week at a resort for our anniversary, and this is our confirmation and informational packet."

"Desire Resorts?" she questioned. "What kind of resort is that?" I could tell her wheels were turning. Maybe she was wondering about it for herself and Sully. With as much ogling he did of my ass any time he saw me outside, I'd venture he would love a place like Desire Resorts.

"It's for...swingers," I told her matter-of-factly. I wasn't much for subterfuge. Besides, I already knew all the neighbors had their suspicions about us, and I couldn't care less what they thought.

She smiled and told me to have a nice day, then she headed back toward her home. I ripped open the envelope to take a look. I'd have to hide it until I found the right time to reveal my surprise to David!

"Daddy, where are you going?" Aubrey asked as David slipped on his sneakers and began stretching his legs.

"The new neighbor asked me to play basketball with him and some of the guys," David answered.

Aubrey shrugged and went back to watch *Frozen* for the approximately four billionth time. My ears perked at the sound of "the guys." This I had to see. I waited an appropriate amount of time for the fellas to settle into their game, then just happened to sashay myself out to the porch in my bikini top and tiny cut-off denim shorts to check out the scene.

Sure enough, there were six guys in the street, right in the cul-de-sac. I wasn't sure if they could see me, but I was close enough to spy on them, especially with my large black sunglasses. Our new next door neighbor, who was a tall drink of water with dark skin and perfect hair, was playing with Sully, the neighbor who always gawks at me, and some other handsome guy. The other team was made up of Greer, the hot single dad, Phillip, one of the older neighbors on the other side of the street, and David.

There was quite a bit of jostling for the ball, some intense checking, probably a foul here and there, and more made shots than I would have guessed for a street pick-up game. *Did I mention the palpable smell of testosterone in the air?*

I had already thought about trying to bring Greer over to the dark side, but now our new neighbor Erik was piquing my interest as well. I did what any respectable hostess would do and went inside to grab some snacks and drinks.

I noticed a few other wives congregating around the cul-de-sac to cheer their husbands on. It looked like they brought out a cooler too. I'd always found the other ladies on the street to be a little standoffish, but I remembered what David had said about trying to make friends with the neighbors. I was trying my best!

I wondered if Jayne, Phillip's wife, or Nina, Sully's wife, would notice if I flirted with Greer and Erik, and whoever that hottie was with Erik. The wonderful thing about this whole swinger lifestyle was that David didn't mind if I flirted. In fact, he enjoyed it. He'd already confided that to me after our first swinger party. He loved watching me interact with Evan. He had really been looking forward to the threesome with Derek too. *Stupid douchebag*. Derek, of course, not my darling hubby!

After the game, David brought Sully and Phil over to see our progress with the basement renovations. Apparently they had seen the contractor's truck in our driveway earlier in the week and wanted to know what was up. I would have loved to have seen the story David concocted for them as to why we were renovating our basement with so many bedrooms, but I needed to get ready for our date that night. We were headed out with Joel and Katie, who were apparently over the fact that we knew her parents.

After I showered, shaved and redid my makeup, I scoured my closet for the perfect dress. I pulled out a slinky skin-tight black dress that was basically no more than a tube of fabric. It looked pretty innocuous on the hanger, but once it was wrapped around my curves, it took on a life of its own. David called it my magic dress because it was so misleading when you saw it off.

I headed into the kitchen to check on Aidan and Aubrey, who were finishing up the fish sticks and macaroni and cheese I made for them. And peas. God, you'd think I was trying to force-feed them arsenic or something. The forlorn spoonfuls of peas rested on their plates untouched.

"Eat your peas, kids," I chided them as I headed for the door.

"Or what?" Aidan yelled back.

"Or I'll tell Ms. Watson you can't have any dessert or snacks tonight," I warned him. Denying my kids sugar was like denying a drug addict of their next high.

Aidan knew Jenna well enough to know she was a stickler for the rules. She was a teacher, after all. Sure enough, he began scooping up peas one at a time, holding his nose and then swallowing them like a pill so he wouldn't have to taste them. *Hey, whatever it takes*, I thought to myself as I slipped on my dangerously high leopard-print platform sandals.

"Hey, I've gotta go check something," I said after a strange twinge gripped my lower abdomen. It felt like a cramp. The kids were too busy gagging on peas to give me much of a response.

I hightailed it into the bathroom where David was taking a shower. Of course it was filled with steam, which immediately began fucking up my makeup. "What's wrong?" he asked when he heard me groan. I sat down on the toilet and prayed to whatever higher power is in charge of menstruation, begging for that twinge I felt not to be a cramp.

"Nothing, honey," I answered. "Just gotta pee." I grabbed a few sheets of toilet paper and wiped, keeping my mental fingers crossed. Holding my breath, I glanced down and was relieved to see no streak of red. I washed my hands and rushed back to the kitchen to supervise the pea consumption. *Gotta keep the kids honest.*

"Did you finish yours already?" I asked Aidan, with my eyebrow raised. He was a sneaky kid sometimes; I wouldn't be surprised if I found those blasted peas in the trash or hidden in a potted plant or something.

He nodded with a grin on his face. "But I don't understand why I have to go to Ms. Watson's house tonight. Why can't I go hang out with my friends instead?"

"Mrs. Garrett is out of town this weekend, honey," I answered. I actually didn't know if she was, but I had forgotten to ask her earlier in the week. But I had gone over to Jenna's house on Thursday to beg her to babysit tonight, as soon as I got the confirmation from Joel and Katie that we could get it on. When I showed up over there, apparently Jenna was getting ready for a hot date. This smokin' guy showed up on a motorcycle to pick her up.

Maybe our cute little divorcée is finally getting her groove back! He looked a little wild. Maybe they would want to hook up with us? Our hot tub is pretty damn persuasive...

"Why do you and Daddy go out every weekend?" Aubrey complained, looking up from her plate, where she was moving her peas from one side to the other. My maternal instincts told me once those peas crossed into the enemy territory of leftover cheese sauce from the macaroni and cheese, there was no way they would ever pass her lips, let alone make the journey into her stomach.

"Because we're adults, and adults need time to play with other adults, the same way kids need time to play with other kids," I retorted as if I had that answer all prepared and stored away to use precisely for this type of situation.

She pursed her lips and squinted her eyes for a moment as if she were testing the validity of my statement. She seemed satisfied, then a worried look creeped across her face. "My birthday is on a Saturday this year," she said. How she knew that, I had no freakin' clue. "Will you leave us with a babysitter on my birthday?"

The fact she would even ask that caused a pang to my heart. "Oh, honey, no, of course not! We will be celebrating your birthday just like we do every year!"

"Good! Because I want to have a slumber party!" Her face brightened and her mouth, a perfect replica of mine, spread into a wide grin.

Okay, so maybe I'm never going to be Mom of the Year, but I ain't half bad.

AFTER DINNER, WE GOT JOEL AND KATIE RIGHT WHERE WE wanted them. Right in the hot tub, with that sexy, bubbling water percolating all around our naked bodies. Joel took the seat next to me, immediately putting his arm around me after I made a show of getting in nice and slowly so he could get a good look at my curvy ass. *You know what? I may not be model thin, but I have a nice rack and a booty you could set your drink on, and you better believe I'm gonna flaunt the hell out of them.*

"You are so fucking sexy, Valley," Joel whispered in my ear as I settled into his outstretched arm, leaning my head against him. I looked across the hot tub where Katie, a gorgeous, long-legged redhead had one leg propped up on the bench seat and the other extended over David's body where his dexterous fingers worked on massaging her from calf to hip. They looked to be getting along very well.

This is finally going to happen.

After all this time—more than a month on the swinger site and since meeting Ed and Shawna—we were finally going to have a full swap. Joel and Katie made it pretty clear at dinner that they were expecting us to go all the way. Our basement was still unusable for swinging activities, but we were prepared to take them up to our bedroom after our steamy soak.

Hey, whatever it takes, right?

Joel reached for my hand, pulling it into his lap where his impressive erection jutted up proudly. I wrapped my fingers around it and gave a tiny squeeze, loving the look in his eyes as the steam from the hot tub billowed around him. He stroked his fingers down my face as we turned toward each other, my hand still slowly stroking his cock up and down.

"God, I want you so bad," he said right before his lips brushed against mine.

"So I can feel," I whispered back as he began to devour me with his mouth, tasting of the sweet Moscato I'd poured for all of us.

This was only the third man I'd kissed in the lifestyle, and he was an even better kisser than Evan or Derek (a.k.a. Mr. Douchebag I Never Heard From Again). His lips were soft, but firm, with just the right amount of resistance. I appreciated the fact that he didn't shove his tongue down my throat, but rather took his time, nibbling at me and gently licking the seam of my lips to wordlessly ask me to part them.

I broke away after a moment, just to glance at David and see how things were going on his end. No matter what happened, I felt a sense of obligation to make sure he was enjoying himself. We'd already vowed not to "take one for the team." If either of us felt uncomfortable at any time, then game over.

But he looked to be equally excited as Joel, his own cock engorged as he kissed Katie and threaded his hands through her beautiful auburn hair. Knowing another woman made him hard didn't make me jealous. It was a fucking turn on, actually.

Knowing he was going to fuck her and then come to bed with me gave me a rush. I couldn't wait to see him slide into her pussy, watch his face react to the feel of her wrapped around his cock, and hear the moans she elicited from him.

Joel took my distraction as a signal to ramp things up a notch. Grabbing me by the hips, he lifted me up and threw me on top of him so that I sank down onto his cock. Not inside me, of course, but damn I could feel the tip of it throbbing against my pussy lips. Never have I ever wanted a cock inside me so badly. Well, I probably have, but in those cases I would have just grabbed it and shoved it in. Obviously, being in the hot tub, we weren't going to be able to go any further. We'd have to get inside and wrangle a condom on that thing before proceeding.

I hadn't been with another man since I was in college, before I met David. That's a long fucking time with one cock. I didn't know why the prospect excited me so much, if it was the novelty or the taboo of it, or even the fact

David would be watching. Whatever the reasons, I was ready to bask in the exhilarating wickedness of it, to celebrate the consummation our hedonistic odyssey.

Joel captured my lips with his again, creating more steam between us than the hot tub ever thought of producing. His hands were all over me, cupping my breasts, wrapped around me, pulling me down on top of him so he could feel my weight against his desire. He stroked his fingers down my back, his desperation to be inside me communicated loud and clear.

But it was David who broke away from Katie to address our intimate group. "Why don't we move this up to the bedroom?" I had a feeling no one would argue. They didn't.

We were silent, only the sounds of our bodies slipping out of the water, rolling splashes, and the sound of the jets shutting off. Joel helped David place the cover back over the tub, and the moonlight highlighted all the delicious planes of their bodies.

Joel was muscular, a bit stockier than David, his cock thicker but shorter. David was all long and lean, a cock to match. I had a momentary vision of me on my knees with both of those scrumptious pieces of manmeat between me, going back and forth, licking, sucking, teasing. A wave of excitement passed over me, knowing it could actually happen...and soon.

"Towels are over here on the patio table," I broke the silence. I handed one to each of my guests, then to my husband, taking one for myself last.

I loved the way the cool night air felt evaporating the water from my body, sending steam into the atmosphere and tightening my nipples into firm buds. I dried off and led my entourage inside and up the stairs to the main floor of the house.

"I'm just going to use the bathroom really quickly," I announced, ushering everyone else into our bedroom. Three towel-wrapped bodies nodded and went inside as I let myself into the bathroom in the hallway. I figured Katie could use the ensuite bathroom if she needed to.

I settled myself down on the toilet to empty my bladder, realizing how engorged my pussy still was, and how sensitive. I had a momentary strike of nervousness flutter through me, but it was quickly replaced with pure anticipation, the good kind.

I went to wipe, then glanced down just in time to see... a fucking red streak of blood on the toilet paper.

What the actual fuck?

Fury coursed through me like magma through a volcano, so intensely that I began to shake with rage. Fuck, what was I going to tell them? What was I going to do?

How could my body pick this exact moment to start my period? It's like some sort of cosmic conspiracy to cockblock me!

I flushed the toilet, grabbed a tampon from under the sink, then washed my hands. I couldn't stop the word "fuck" from forming on my lips over and over again, as if it was on automatic repeat in my brain. Then I marched into the bedroom and asked David if he could come out into the hall.

"What's wrong?" He looked genuinely concerned. I felt terrible because I was about to cockblock him too.

"You're not going to fucking believe this," I began, watching his eyebrows quirk with panic. He already knew just from looking at me that something was indeed wrong and that he wasn't going to like it.

"Just tell me, Valley," he said, trying to make his voice calm and light but failing miserably.

"I just started my motherfucking period." I stood there with my hands on my hips, enraged by the injustice of the universe.

"Oh, shit." He glanced around as if there would be another solution floating about he could grasp onto. "So that means we can't play?" It only sounded like half a question as it hung in the air, waiting for my response.

My head swiveled in a little shake while my shoulders shrugged. "I guess you can if you want." *No! No! No!*, my brain shouted. *That is not what you want.* But it was too late; I'd already put the words out there.

He scoffed. "I'm not playing without you, Valley."

This. This is why I love my husband so much.

He really is a team player, and I knew in my heart of hearts he wouldn't let me down. There was no way I would even attempt this lifestyle if I didn't know that would be his answer. I let out a deep sigh, and he pulled me to his chest, squeezing me against his still-damp body.

"There will be other times," he said, kissing the top of my head.

"Well, let's go break the news," I finally said. He wrapped his arm around my shoulder and guided me through the threshold of our bedroom.

"I have a plumbing issue," I announced. "Mother Nature just decided to pay me a visit early."

Katie's face instantly fell, her expectant smile swallowed up by a frown. I wasn't sure if Joel would understand my euphemisms, but his face also dropped. I was trying to cover up my anger with sarcasm, but it was obvious I was furious. I've never been good at hiding my feelings.

Katie stood up and pulled me into a hug. I wrapped my arms around her small body and felt myself heave with a few shallow sobs. *No*, I screamed at myself. *I'm not going to cry because I got my period!* But the hormones were making it impossible to tamp down my out-of-control wildfire of emotions.

"This happens all the time," she whispered into my hair. "I had to cancel our playdate last weekend for that very reason, as a matter of fact."

"I'm so sorry," I blubbered.

Joel rose off the bed and came over to where his wife and I were standing, locked in an embrace. He tapped Katie's shoulder, and when she pulled away, he took me into his arms.

"I wanted you so bad," I sniffled.

He chuckled a bit and squeezed me tightly to his body. "Damn, woman, you have no idea how bad I wanted to fuck you."

He wasn't hard anymore. *Too bad, or I might have given him a BJ anyway.* I hated sending my guests home with blue balls. That wasn't the type of hostess I wanted to be!

"We'll have another chance soon, I promise," he assured me, giving me a soft kiss on my cheek.

I was relieved they were so understanding. *I guess no one can be too angry at Mother Nature. I mean, she kinda does what she wants.* After we all got dressed, David and I walked them down the hall and to the foyer, where we said goodbye with kisses and promises to try again soon.

After they left, we walked over to Jenna's to pick up

the kids. She seemed surprised that we were back so soon, and had fully anticipated keeping our little angels overnight. But it was only 10 PM, and I couldn't imagine imposing upon her if it wasn't necessary. They were watching a movie in her family room, but Aidan especially seemed relieved to see us.

After we got them tucked into bed, we retired to our own room. I snuggled myself down in David's arms, soothing what remained of my disappointment. "I can't believe we're almost two months into this, and I haven't even gotten fucked yet."

He chuckled. "I know. But it will happen, Valley. We just have to be patient."

"Patience isn't exactly my forte," I reminded him. My mind began wandering over possible scenarios. "Hey, that next door neighbor is pretty hot. And single, I think. Maybe I should invite him over for a threesome? And maybe that cute friend of his too." My mind began to spin with flashes of what that might entail.

David laughed again. "Valley, he's gay."

"Fuuuuuuuck!" I sighed. "Really?"

I could barely see him in the moonlight coming through the window, but I thought he nodded his head.

"What about that neighbor across the street? Greer?"

"I don't think he's gay, but he seems pretty focused on his daughter."

"Damn it, universe!" The frustration was starting to settle over me again like a dark cloud. "If I had balls, they would be as blue as a Smurf right now!"

Our bedroom erupted with the sound of David laughing his ass off at me. I swatted him and then harrumphed.

"I'm sorry, Valley, but that was hilarious," he finally apologized when his burst of amusement subsided.

He could tell I wasn't nearly as entertained as he was, so he leaned down to press a kiss onto the edge of my lips. "Sweetheart, I love you, and we're going to make this happen sooner or later, okay? We just have to keep trying."

"Okay," I relented, pulling him toward me. I might not have wanted Joel to fuck me while I was having my period, but that didn't mean David was off the hook...

❧ 11 ❧

"**H**ey, before you go, come take a look at this message we got on the site!" David yelled after me as I rushed to get my jewelry and makeup on.

"I don't have time, David. I'm already running late. If they look interesting, can you just reply?"

"I think you're going to like this guy," he called down the hall.

"Shhhhh!" I ran down to the office to poke my head in and remind him to watch himself in front of the kids. I appreciated all the effort he was putting in to finding a couple for us to hook up with, but at this point, I would be surprised if anyone wanted to play with us. It was disappointing too, especially after Ed and Shawna assured us we were a perfect fit for the lifestyle, and after I had so many eyes on me at all the parties we'd been to.

"How long will you be gone?" he questioned, his eyes still glued to the laptop screen.

"No idea. It's the first meeting, so it could either be

short or mind-numbingly long. If that bitch president of the PTA is running it, I'm guessing it will be the latter."

"Damn," he lamented. "Well, I'll be here when you get home."

We'd hardly seen each other lately. He was always rushing off to some planning meeting for this new church project. The board was being completely anal about being involved in every single minute detail of designing the church building. So far he'd met with a half-dozen small groups: the music people, the children's staff, the persnickety old biddies who donated the most money, and God (literally) knows who else.

Throughout it all, David had maintained his positive, professional demeanor. I don't know how he does it. I would have told them all to go to hell at this point. *Guess it's pretty obvious I don't belong in their church, huh?*

Tonight was the first meeting for the Sunview Elementary Media Center Re-launch. That was seriously what Mrs. Emily Walters titled it on the fancy faux-leather binders she'd mailed to our homes earlier this week. Apparently she couldn't just wait until we got there tonight to hand them to us in person. No, she needed to send them in advance because we had homework: memorizing every excruciating detail of the crap in the binders. My fucking name was even embossed on the front. *Not even fucking kidding.*

At least Jenna would be there. She, of course, would be there in her official capacity as teacher, but I looked forward to at least one person not giving me the evil eye as soon as I walked in the door. *I think Jenna would consider herself to be my friend?* And from what I saw of that dude who picked her up for a date last week, I'd say she has a much bigger bad girl streak than I gave her credit for. *Maybe I'll lure her into our bedroom after all!*

I arrived at the school about five minutes late and sauntered in, taking my time. I tried to dress conservatively in a little sundress with a crocheted shrug thrown over it for coverage. I looked down to see my cleavage hanging out like nobody's business. *I can't help it if the girls just don't want to be ignored. They tend to push themselves into the limelight no matter what I do, attention whores that they are.*

I could survey the scene in the old media center before entering due to the all-glass walls. Emily Walters was perched behind the podium with her nose all scrunched up like she'd just smelled a nasty fart or something. Her normally kinky-curly auburn hair was piled on top of her head in a perfectly formed bun, and seeing her there, I don't know why it never occurred to me before that she was the perfect archetype of an old maid librarian. If she weren't married and a mother, I was sure she'd be an obnoxiously shushing librarian who went home every night to her bookcase-lined dungeon guarded by a legion of cats. Even so, I was pretty sure her coochy had dried out from lack of use not long after she popped her second kid out.

As soon as she spotted me entering the doors, she called out to the rest of the moms and teachers in attendance, "Oh, good, Mrs. Archer finally decided to join us! I guess we can get things underway."

I rolled my eyes as I took a seat not far from Jenna, but she was with her teacher friends and didn't even smile at me. *Wow, I'm even shunned by the neighbor. That's just awesome.*

Two hours and fifteen minutes later, I wearily dragged my ass out of the uncomfortable plastic chair and across the ugly, worn carpet of the media center. Apparently I was being put in charge of picking out new carpet, along with paint colors, curtains, furniture, lighting and whatever else "would contribute to the overall aesthetic," as Emily so snobbily dictated.

I was probably going to kill that woman before this was all said and done. Oh, and of course, I was doing it all *pro bono* because apparently I owed the school a favor for letting my kids go there. Just a sneaky way for the PTA to save big on their budget.

As I headed out the main doors to the parking lot, I heard my name echo down the empty hallway. It seemed like most of the moms and other teachers were going to hang out and dish about the latest Starbuck's drink or something, but I was so outta there as soon as Ms. Cobweb Coochy adjourned it.

I whipped around to see Jenna padding along behind me. "Hey, Valley," she said as she approached.

"Looks like we both survived…this time," I said, rolling my eyes.

"No doubt. That was brutal."

"Who's watching your kids tonight?" I asked as we crossed the parking lot.

"Oh, Mike has them all month. It's summer break and all," she answered. "Time to sow my wild oats!"

"I bet you were sowing something the other night with Mr. Biker dude!" I teased her. "He was seriously hot."

A blush crept across her face. "Uh…yeah."

I was hoping she'd divulge a few more details. Her face told me it hadn't gone that well, but she remained tight-lipped. "Well, guess I better get home to my crew," I said as I reached my car.

"Guess we should have ridden together," she said with a shrug. "Don't know why I didn't think of it."

"That's okay. Maybe next time." I smiled warmly to reinforce the fact I hoped we could be friends. *Yes, yes, whether or not it would get us in her pants. See, I'm not all about sex.*

"Sounds like there are going to be plenty of next times." She sighed heavily.

"Next time we'll go out drinking afterwards," I suggested, giving her a wink.

"Sounds like a plan!" She winked back as she climbed into her car.

Apparently I *wasn't* hated by all non-lifestyle women. It felt like a small victory, and at that point, I'd take what I could get.

WHEN I GOT HOME, THE KIDS WERE ALREADY IN BED, WHICH was surprising since they had just gotten out of school for the summer. They usually conned us into letting them stay up way too late in the summertime, which meant our adult time was as rare as diamonds. David put his finger to his lips as soon as I walked in from the garage and slammed my stupid faux-leather binder down on the countertop in the kitchen.

"I want to show you something," he said, taking my hand and guiding me toward his office.

He was positively glowing with excitement. I hadn't seen him this excited since I scored us tickets to see U2 when they came to town. "What is it, honey?" I asked. *I'm not terribly into the whole being surprised thing. I would rather just know what's going to happen.*

He sat down at his desk and navigated to the website, then to our inbox. "Here. I made us a date for later this week."

"Wow, really?" I asked, scanning the inbox at the list of messages that had been exchanged. "When? What about the kids?"

When he grinned that broadly, I always saw the little boy he used to be. He looked exactly like Aidan with his lips stretched like that. "I arranged for my parents to take the kids for a whole week!"

"What?" My body was suddenly flooded with excitement, like he'd magically transferred his excitement into my body. "Are you serious?"

He nodded vigorously. "Yup, and I took a few days off work too. It's been a long time since we've had the house to ourselves for a day or two. It's summertime, and there's plenty for the kids to do over at my parents' house."

My brows quirked. "There is? Like what?"

"Well, my mom said something about Vacation Bible School and some activities at the local park—a day camp or something."

"VBS, huh?" I snickered at the irony of my kids going to church while David and I were getting it on with strangers in our secret swinger lair.

He nodded again. "Yeah, and I thought we'd get the plans for the basement finalized too so we can throw a huge party at the end of the summer."

"Wow, honey, I am so excited and so impressed that you came up with this all by yourself!" I threw my arms around his neck as I leaped onto his lap, straddling him. He pushed off the desk and spun us around in his rolling chair until we almost went flying off. I had such a rush; I hadn't been felt this carefree and in love with my husband since...well, probably not since our last child-free getaway. But it had been a year or two since that.

"So let's check out this couple, okay?" he asked as we came to a stop. He navigated to their profile, then rose from the chair so I could take the reins.

I immediately liked what I saw. For once, this wasn't some waify Victoria Secret model-type woman. She was thick with full breasts and a bit of a pooch around her tummy, not unlike me. He was broad and muscular with a bald head and a big diamond stud in each ear. They were in their early forties, on their second marriage with no kids in the house, and they seemed to be very experienced judging by the number of testimonials they had on their page. Everyone agreed they were an amazing couple well worth meeting.

"They're really yummy, David, well done!" I commended him as I glanced up to see his eyes still dancing with excitement. He had a new emotion reflecting from his hazel eyes now, though: one of pride.

"They're coming over on Wednesday; I thought we'd grill out dinner, then hang out in the hot tub. What do you think?"

I gave him a huge smooch right on the lips. "I think I married the most awesome man in the world, that's what I think!"

IT WAS ONE OF THOSE DAYS WHERE EVERYTHING SEEMED TO be getting away from me. I was trying to clean the house to prepare for our company, post my daily blog content, and pack the kids' things to take to their grandparents' house for the week. Plus I had a pie in the oven, and no, that's not some sort of weird euphemism for a crazy sex act (unfortunately).

I was just about to lose my mind when the doorbell rang. I had already dealt with the contractor coming to measure stuff for the basement, the UPS man (who was hot, by the way) delivering a package (also not a euphemism), and some other interruption that I couldn't even remember now.

"For fuck's sake, what now?" I clasped my hand over my mouth when I realized I said the F word out loud. Aidan was out of the house, over playing with the Garrett boys down the street, but Aubrey was sitting at the kitchen counter brushing her doll's hair and sticking approximately four hundred barrettes to the poor thing's head.

I rushed toward the door, feeling more frazzled than I ever let myself get, and swung it open to reveal the sweet neighbor from across the street, Posey. *Wait. That's whose house Aidan is at.* And there was Aidan peeking out from behind Posey's small frame. For a moment there I thought I really had lost my mind.

I ushered them both inside with a sinking feeling as to why she was chaperoning my son back to our house. I figured he'd done or said something inappropriate. *Great.* Just what I wanted to do was send him off to his grandparents' house grounded for the week.

"What's wrong?" I questioned, searching Posey's face

for clues. Aidan was looking incredibly sheepish, and Posey's boys weren't in tow, so I had no idea. She was clutching a small plastic grocery sack in her hand that was tied in a knot at the top. I couldn't tell what was inside—cucumbers maybe? Maybe she was bringing me some produce from her garden?

"Aidan, I'm going to talk to your mother for a moment," Posey said with a lightness to her voice, like my son wasn't in serious trouble.

"Go see what Aubrey is up to," I directed him. He shrugged and dashed off, seemingly relieved to be off the hook. I turned to Posey, not able to handle the suspense any longer. "What's going on?"

She waited to make sure Aidan was no longer within earshot, then she lifted the sack toward me as if it contained dog doo. *I guess that means it's not cucumbers?* I still found it impossible to determine what the hell was going on from the expression on her face, which was a mix of amusement and embarrassment.

"I think these belong to you," she said, her eyes twinkling as a smile curled her lips up.

"What is it?" I still felt completely clueless.

"Uh…toys?" She shoved the bag into my hand as though she was grateful to be rid of it. "Uh…sex toys?"

Oh god, no.

"The boys were pretending they were death ray guns," she explained with a little headshake. "First I had to give them a lecture about how guns are not toys. Then I had to explain that these particular items are not guns—they are adult toys."

I tried to keep from laughing, but was finding it nearly impossible to contain my giggling. "What did they say?"

"Uh, I don't think they really understood…but they did seem a bit mortified when I promised they'd understand someday." She gave a little wink to show she wasn't upset. Well, at least that was a relief. What kind of mother's vibrators get stolen and used at the neighbor's house as death ray guns? *Sigh. I guess I'm that mom.* At least he didn't take them to school. Emily Walters would've never let me hear the end of that.

"As you can imagine, with our house being a cop's home, we take gun safety pretty seriously," she continued, the merriment fading from her features.

I nodded. "Of course." I still felt just awful about what happened to her husband. "Thanks for bringing them back over," I said as I heard a car door slam in the driveway. I assumed David was home early from work to see the kids off when his parents arrived to pick them up for their week-long stay.

I was still holding the plastic sack of sex toys when my in-laws strutted right up the steps of our porch until they stopped at the glass door Posey and I stood behind. "Oh," Posey said, tilting her head toward the door. "Looks like you have company! Let me get out of your hair."

I used every muscle in my entire body to restrain myself from rolling my eyes. My in-laws had arrived early. Not just a little early, like two hours early. I didn't have anything packed, and I was standing in my foyer holding a bag of dildos. *Perfect.* I sighed as I pushed the door open so David's parents could join our lovely tête-à-tête about gun safety and vibrators.

"What's going on here?" David's mother snarled with her hoity-toity eyebrow quirked high on her face.

"Oh, nothing," my neighbor replied, extending her

hand politely. "I'm Posey Garrett from across the street. It's nice to meet you!"

Joanna nodded with a bored expression on her face. That woman was such a miserable bitch. How did she really squeeze my amazing husband out of her old, dried-up coochy? You'd think she'd pop out another miserable bitch, one like Emily Walters, for example.

"What's in the bag, Valley?" my mother-in-law questioned, her eyes digging into me like they had sharp hooks on them. She had this painful way of judging me, even before getting the answers to her questions.

"Nothing, Joanna. You know you're early to get the kids, right?"

She said nothing, but I could tell Posey felt sorry for me. She shrank back from David's parents, excusing herself again, then flashed me a look that said *Good luck with that!*

Good luck, indeed!

The electricity firing across the table as we dug into our barbecued feast was palpable. While Joe and Sandy looked a bit older than the photos they had posted on the website, they were a really warm, friendly couple, and still quite attractive. I wasn't sure if I bought that they were in their early forties—they looked more like late forties, but hey, at this point I wasn't going to be picky.

How many couples had we been out with now? Besides Ed and Shawna, Evan and Hailey, and Joel and Katie, there had been a few others between failed dates and parties that didn't pan out. Not that we weren't planning to see Joel and Katie again when they got back from vacation, but I had the distinct feeling tonight was the night I would lose my swinger virginity. *Finally.*

David was glancing at me in between looks at Sandy. She was a curvy, dark-haired beauty, not unlike an older version of myself, though not quite as tall. She had a cute, upturned nose and gorgeous dark eyes framed by frilly lashes. Her laugh was sparkling and her wit, sharp—she'd already fired off a few one-liners that had our entire table roaring with laughter. Plus she'd put away three glasses of wine already, and I could tell that she was beyond suggestible. Not to mention the fact she was looking at my husband as if he were a hunk of meat. *In a good way, of course.*

The light was beaming off Joe's freshly-shaved scalp. I'd never touched a bald head before, and I was anxious to know what it would feel like to run my fingers across it in the throes of passion. He also had a thick, bushy goatee, and I couldn't help but wonder what it might feel like tickling me as he delved into my nether regions. Joe was much more quiet than his wife, but he had a deep, sexy voice that vibrated through the whole room when he finally did speak, and what little he had to say was articulate and smart.

"So how did you guys get into the lifestyle?" David asked as he speared another chunk of his steak with his fork. I flashed him a warning not to eat too much; sex and full stomachs don't mix.

"We met in on a lifestyle cruise, what, six years ago now, honey?" Sandy answered, glancing at her husband for confirmation.

He nodded and wiped his mouth. "We'd both been in

the lifestyle with our exes and had gone on the cruise to celebrate our divorces being finalized."

"Yeah, we had no clue we'd come back well on our way to getting hitched!" Sandy laughed as the memories reflected from her eyes. "We were both bound and determined to live it up as singles for a while, but I guess the Man Upstairs had other plans. We were destined to be together."

"Aww, that's so sweet, guys!" I cooed. "Much sexier, too, than our story of meeting in college stats class."

"You just never know where love will find you," Sandy agreed. She raised her glass toward her husband, who clinked his against hers with a grin and a wink.

It was really nice to see a couple who got along so well. Before we tried the whole lifestyle thing, I'd always assumed couples who went down this road had marital issues. But what we had learned so far was that lifestyle couples were far happier than vanilla ones. And I felt like we were well on our way to joining the exclusive club!

After a beat, David asked, "Is anyone interested in getting in the hot tub tonight?"

Sandy's eyes lit up like she thought we'd never ask. I rose from the table and began stacking our dishes, and she and Joe helped me carry them to the kitchen while David went downstairs to take the cover off the tub. Excitement vibrated through me as I promised our guests the dishes could wait until later. I wanted to be percolating in that tub within the next ten minutes.

I ushered them downstairs into what was slowly becoming our swinger lair. There was still quite of bit of work to be done, but David was confident we'd be throwing parties in there by the end of the summer. I had my heart set on a Labor Day weekend party.

"Looks like you're doing a bit of remodeling here," Joe observed, glancing around at the 2x4s framing out the bedrooms and the bigger bathroom area.

"Yes, and I'm sorry the bathroom down here is out of commission. I probably should have asked you to change upstairs before coming down here," I apologized. I had a stack of towels in my arms for use after the tub, but I had forgotten about the getting from Point A, clothed and dry, to Point B, naked and wet, part.

"I don't need no stinkin' bathroom to change," Sandy said, her face bright with confidence. Just like that, she reached behind herself, unzipped her dress and let it fall into a puddle around her feet. She was wearing absolutely *zero* items of clothing under the dress.

It definitely appeared that she had had her breasts done. They were a lot perkier than mine, and very tan, with big white triangles over her nipples where her bikini top must have been for most of the summer. "We have a boat," she explained. "And as much as I'd love to be out there naked all the time, Joe thinks it might cause a boating accident or something!"

I laughed and David, who joined us from the patio, quipped, "I can definitely see why he's concerned!" He moved behind Sandy and stroked his hands down her ample curves, then lowered his lips to press a soft kiss against her bronze shoulder.

"I guess it's my turn!" I said, unzipping my own dress and sliding it over my head. My hips were too big for it to go the other way. I was wearing a gorgeous coral lace bra and matching thong underneath. I watched Joe as I shed my first layer of material, and it's safe to say his jaw dropped. He literally looked too stunned to speak after I stood there prancing about in my pretty lace undergarments.

David took the lull in conversation as a signal to drop trou, and then we were just waiting for Joe to make his move. He did take off his pants, but left his boxers on, sort of like Evan had when he and Hailey were over for our inaugural dip with another couple. I didn't think anything of it until we got out to the patio and we all got in the bubbling pot of goodness. Then Joe turned around, aiming his ass right in my face and wiggled out of his boxer shorts before covertly slipping in beside me. It was all done so swiftly, I didn't get a look at his body at all, except for a flash of tattoos.

He had extensive artwork all over his arms and back. There was a dragon and something tribal-looking, and maybe Chinese symbols. It was hard to tell in the constantly shifting colors. The moonlight bounced off his bald head as he swept me into his arms quite handily, aided by the weightlessness effect of the water. I ended up in his lap right before his lips sealed over mine, swallowing the squeal the surprise of his action elicited.

He was a rough kisser, lots of biting and nipping, which was fine. I liked aggressive men. Sometimes I found David to be a little too gentle, so I started to wonder if I was in for a real treat with a dominant type of guy. I mean, he did have that whole look with the bald head and earrings, so maybe I should have expected it.

I pressed against him, thinking any moment I would feel his erection rise to jab into my stomach or thighs, depending on his size and which way he hung. One of the most exciting aspects of this whole adventure for me was unwrapping that best of gifts and getting a glimpse of what might be in store for me. Now if I could just move beyond third base… I had a feeling, though, that tonight was going to be a home run!

I started to contemplate how baseball really lent itself to sexual references when I heard Sandy begin to moan. I glanced over to see that David had lifted her up onto the edge of the tub, and he had his face buried in her crotch. *Well, hot damn!* It was nice seeing him pushing boundaries and moving us forward. And Sandy seemed to be enjoying every single tongue-lash. *What can I say? I trained him well.*

I decided I should follow suit. I wanted to maintain my reputation as hostess with the mostest, after all. I nudged Joe and gestured for him to sit on the edge of the hot tub opposite his wife so he could watch her in the throes of ecstasy while I sucked his cock. He certainly did not object.

I perched myself on the bench and rested my elbows on his thighs so I could be in the perfect position to pleasure him. He had a mass of thick pubes, which I found a little odd as most lifestyle folks kept themselves neatly groomed south of the border. I tried not to let that deter me though as I stroked my fingers down the sides of his leg and ran my tongue down his shaft.

He was not erect when I started, but I assumed I'd have him raring to go in no time. I was a little disappointed that seeing me naked and making out with me hadn't gotten him that excited, but I tried not to take it personally. *Guys get nervous sometimes, right?* I realized they weren't always as in control of their penises as they'd have us believe.

The licking didn't seem to be doing anything for him, so I just sucked the whole thing into my mouth and began to deepthroat him, which wasn't too challenging considering his lack of size or hardness. I am not one to give up, and he did seem to be enjoying it. His head was tossed back and his mouth partly open, from which deep groans rumbled out at regular intervals. I reached up with one of my hands and cupped his balls. Remembering how aggressive he'd been with me, I even fondled them a little roughly, thinking maybe it just took more pressure to get him going.

Still nothing.

I had noticed he had a silver hoop coming out of each nipple. This was my first time seeing a man with his nipples pierced in person, though I had seen some photos of the phenomenon on the swinger site. He obviously liked them played with, or he wouldn't have gone through the trouble of sticking needles through them, right? So I reached up with my other hand and gave one of the small rings a tug, which made him cry out sharply. It sounded like a pleasurable yelp, and he didn't stop me, so I kept up with all three activities.

I was beginning to feel like a multi-handed, multi-tasking robot when I heard an orgasm rip from Sandy's throat and pierce the still air. I gave a fleeting thought to whether or not Erik, our new next door neighbor, heard her cry out, but then I decided I didn't really give a shit.

After Sandy came down from her high, David stood up, and his own impressive hard-on jutted out proudly in front of him. He reached down and took it in his hand, stroking it slowly back and forth as he waited for me to turn and make eye contact with him. I let go of Joe's dick, which was still limp as a wet noodle, and met my husband's gaze. He didn't need to say anything. He was ready to go upstairs.

Well, maybe Joe will have an easier time upstairs in our air-conditioned bedroom, I rationalized. It was a warm evening, and the hot tub, though we didn't keep it terribly hot since it was summer, was still pretty toasty. I figured he might be having issues due to the heat. I resigned myself to trying again upstairs, or maybe he'd even want to reciprocate a bit. *Perhaps my reactions would turn him on?*

We dried off and made our way upstairs to the bedroom, which I'd prepared with a scented candle, a bowl of condoms and perfectly fluffed pillows. I was just about to install a mini fridge up there to make sure we would all stay hydrated, but David assured me that was overkill. "Don't worry, we'll put a fridge in the basement for that very purpose," he promised.

I dropped my towel so Joe could have a good look at my body as I slithered seductively up onto the bed. I tried to do it gracefully, but our bed is kind of high. *Oh, well, at least I have long legs.* I affixed my eyes to his, which seemed to light up as he raked his gaze over my lush curves.

Okay, good, this is going to be fine after all, I told myself.

I didn't have to worry about David. He and Sandy were already lip-locked and pretzeled together on the bed next to us. I think Sandy was preparing to return the oral favor as Joe took one of my nipples into his mouth.

He was as aggressive with my nips as he had been with my lips, and I had to politely direct him to back off a bit. *I like my nipples bitten as much as anyone, but I would prefer to keep them attached to my breasts, thank you very much!*

After only a few more kisses, I noticed he was reaching

to the side of me, his hand in the bowl of condoms. He fumbled around with the package, and next thing I knew he was pressing his semi-erect cock against my pussy, trying to work his way inside.

Only he wasn't really hard.

And since I'd been in the hot tub, I wasn't really all that wet. The hot water had dried me out.

Fuck! What am I supposed to do?

My brain was scrambling for answers. I had a little panic attack until he slid down my body, putting his face squarely between my thighs, which he pried open a little forcefully with his big, thick hands. There was no teasing, no subtlety to it at all; he dove right in for my clit as if it was a succulent bone and he was a dog. As he made lots of wet, slurping noises, I glanced over to David, who was so engrossed in enjoying Sandy, he didn't even feel the weight of my eyes on him. I decided not to disturb him.

I guess I'm going to take one for the team after all.

❧ 12 ❦

I was going over some ideas I'd collected for the media center project when David bustled into the office with two steaming mugs of tea. "Trying to pacify me?" I asked him with an eyebrow raised.

"Honey, I just feel so terrible about what happened last night!" he repeated for the four millionth time. Yeah, I know, he was sorry. I didn't blame him, anyway.

"It's not your fault, David. His dick was like a wet noodle." I shrugged and shuddered, trying to erase the image from my mind.

"You should have just told me. I would have stopped. I would have called off the whole thing," he insisted.

I wrapped my arms around him. "Honey, it's fine. You were having too much fun, and I did get enjoyment from watching you."

He bent down to plant a kiss on my lips. "You are the most amazing wife," he said. "I love you so much. And I promise we're not done trying. When we get this basement done, we're having the mother of all swinger parties!"

My eyes lit up. There was nothing I loved more than hosting parties. Some of the ones I threw before we became parents were legendary—and they were just shy of a lifestyle party in scope and scale, *if you catch my drift*. I thought David would agree to a small affair to christen our remodeling project, but it sounded like he was giving me some leverage to throw a bigger soiree than I'd originally planned.

"You wanna know exactly how good of a wife I am?" I asked, waiting to see his eyebrows tweak with curiosity. As soon as I achieved the desired response, I reached into the bottom drawer of the filing cabinet, the one where I stored all my stuff for my interior design business, and pulled out the packet I'd received the other day from Desire Resorts. I handed it to him with a huge, wordless grin plastered on my face.

"What's this?" He flipped it open and scanned the introduction, his eyes growing wider by the second. "Wow, are you serious? Do you want to go?" He shifted his eyes down to me as he waited for my response.

"We're already going!" I revealed. "For our anniversary. I booked an ocean-side suite."

The look of shock on his face was absolutely priceless. He yanked me out of the chair and into his arms as he swirled me around the room. "I was right. You are the most amazing wife ever!"

I HATED TO WASTE A SATURDAY NIGHT WITH A BABYSITTER at a neighborhood party instead of hitting up the house party Ed and Shawna had invited us to, but our neighbors on Juniper Court had all been pretty friendly to us since we moved in the summer before. I was already friends with Jenna and Posey, and though I was pretty sure clique-y Nina Sullivan and Jayne Miller disapproved of me, I couldn't turn down an invitation from Jayne to join in the poolside celebration of her husband's birthday.

Besides, it seemed like a good opportunity to see our hot single neighbors, Erik and Greer, shirtless. I didn't give a flying fuck that Erik was gay. He was still fucking hot. I wasn't getting any cock (besides David's, of course) so eye candy would have to do.

If nothing else, I might finally have the chance to steer Greer toward the dark side. *wink*

The kids were still at David's parents' house, and we hadn't heard much from them all week, so we assumed everything was going smoothly. I FaceTimed with them earlier in the day, so I felt like we could go party with the adults without worrying too much about the spawn. With the week I'd had between the death ray vibrator incident, the limp noodle playdate, and Emily Walters leaving me approximately four dozen messages about issues she had with my designs for the media center, I needed some alcoholic drinks stat.

We moseyed over to the Miller's house, and Jayne instructed us to wait outside on the patio to surprise Phillip, who would be arriving any time. Everything went off without a hitch. Jayne seemed pretty nervous about pulling everything together, and I hoped she could relax and enjoy herself.

It certainly looked like Phillip and the other men from the neighborhood, not to mention the men from Phillip's law office, were enjoying themselves. Who knew Phillip had so many hottie attorney friends?

I felt pretty certain one or two of them had to be life-style friendly, just judging by the way they looked at me. They didn't seem shocked when I brazenly stripped off my bikini top—instead, their expressions indicated they'd spent plenty of time skinny dipping. I was apparently in like-minded company, my favorite type of company, in fact.

I thought David might be annoyed I was flirting so boldly with the male party-goers, but I think he still felt so bad about what had happened with Joe that he dared not say a word. By my fourth margarita, I was feeling divine. As crappy as our swinging adventures were turning out to be, I felt I deserved a night on the wild side.

Guzzling down the icy, fruity concoction, I realized what a mistake it was not to have budgeted for a high-end blender for the basement project.

"You know, we gotta get one of these for Project Paradise," I told him, my words slurring ever so slightly as I nudged my head toward the Miller's sleek stainless steel blender.

"One of what?" His face twisted into a look of befuddlement. "For the huh?"

"A kick-ass blender for the basement!" I clarified. Frozen drinks were a must for our swinger soiree headquarters. "I'll have to add one to my shopping list."

He nodded, then looked across the pool where he apparently saw someone he knew. After they made eye contact, he headed over in that direction to strike up a conversation, leaving me alone.

I went over to Jayne to ask if she needed any help with anything, but she said they were going to be cutting the cake soon, so everything was on track. She also handed me a towel, which made me wonder if she was trying to make me cover up. I slung it over my shoulders so it would slightly obscure the girls.

Later I saw David talking to Posey over at one of the patio tables, so I sauntered over to see how she was doing. "Hey, there, recovered from the death ray gun incident?" I asked, trying to keep from laughing.

She nodded and blushed a bit, looking embarrassed for me to bring it up in front of David. Then Jenna joined us and raised her glass for a toast. "To kid-free weekends!" she exclaimed, and we were all happy to join in with a hearty "Here, here!"

"How are the plans coming along for the media center?" Jenna asked once Posey and David went back to their conversation.

"Oh, you know, Emily hates everything I've sent her so far. She keeps saying she wants it to be colorful. I'm afraid it's going to look like something out of *Sesame Street* if I add any more color." I sigh, feeling my head spin after slurping up the last sip of my icy strawberry margarita.

"I don't envy you, that's for sure," Jenna empathized. "I don't think there's any pleasing Emily. Can you imagine how her husband feels?"

I burst into laughter. I couldn't begin to fathom how Emily and her hubby had managed to conceive two children. I imagined she just laid there like a cold fish every time he wanted some action. Either that or she gave him a list of directorial notes after every session with expectations he couldn't possibly satisfy.

I had lost count of how many drinks I'd consumed, but wow, the Millers sure knew how to throw a party. I hadn't had this much fun since the last house party David and I attended, and though there was close to a zero percent chance of bringing home another couple for the night, I did manage to bump into our neighbor Greer from across the street to ask him what his plans were for later in the evening.

Greer was always reserved when I was around, like he just didn't know what to think of me. I was hoping once he got some liquid courage racing through his veins, he'd be a little more receptive to my advances. But he told me he had to get home to his daughter after the party. "Bummer," I told him and pressed my lips against his cheek. Feeling a light sting of rejection when he barely reacted, I washed it down with yet another margarita.

I must have gotten so drunk after that point that I didn't even remember David dragging me home. I'm a big girl and can hold my liquor pretty well, so I definitely overindulged if my memory was that fuzzy. But hey, at least I felt good. The last thing I remembered was David kissing me on the cheek and tucking me into bed before I drifted off for the night.

I WAS GETTING SO MUCH DONE WITH THE KIDS STILL GONE at their grandparents' house. I had exactly 24 hours left of my Mommycation, and though I had promised Emily I would have some fabric samples ready to show her by our next meeting, I was also taking plenty of breaks to surf the swinger website. We had gotten a message the day before from a really sexy single guy, and I was working on making arrangements to meet him for a drink after David got home from work. Then, if that went well, I planned to invite him back to the hot tub.

We'd just gotten to the point of exchanging phone numbers, and I was trying to figure out the best angle to shoot a selfie. I walked down the hall to the living room, then out onto the patio to try to get the best lighting. I was only wearing a bra, but who cares? *It's not any more revealing than a bikini top, right?* He'd already sent me a titillating photo of his scrumptious package, and it did not appear he was going to have any of the issues I encountered with Joe last week.

As soon as I snapped a photo and sent it on its merry way, I heard a car door slam in the driveway. David was home early. I rushed inside to meet him at the door and perform my daily routine of asking him how his day went and giving him an update about mine.

As soon as I laid eyes on him I knew something was wrong. Horribly wrong. His face was twisted into a scowl, and his eyes were narrowed into thin slits. He slammed his briefcase down on the counter and stomped right past me to the bedroom.

I furrowed my eyebrows. David hardly ever got upset. I couldn't even remember the last time... it might have been when he got mad at Aidan for breaking one of his tools in his workshop. But that had been before we'd moved; that's how long he'd gone without getting angry about anything.

I decided to let him cool off for a moment and change

clothes. I figured a client had done something that annoyed him; usually it was clients changing their minds at the last minute, creating a ton of extra work for him that really got his goat. I took a deep breath and headed into the kitchen where I supposed I should consider what to make for dinner.

After ten minutes, I realized he still hadn't emerged from the bedroom. That didn't seem normal. *Okay, a client had royally pissed him off. Strenuously fucked with him.* I decided to go check on him. I pushed open the bedroom door and found him in the corner of the room, staring out the floor-to-ceiling window that looked out on the backyard.

"David?"

He didn't turn my way or acknowledge me at all, so I moved closer to him, close enough to wrap my arms around his waist. As soon as I made contact with his skin, he flinched.

"What the hell is wrong with you?" I fired away at him.

He whipped around, eyes boring into mine with the firepower of a nuclear bomb. I'd certainly never seen him direct that kind of anger toward me before. He said nothing, but his jaw was firmly set, his lips in a thin, straight line and his fists clenched at his side.

"David, what is going on?" The words slipped out of my mouth, each one wrapped in shock. I had never seen him like this in the nearly fifteen years I'd known him.

"I got fired from the church project," he seethed, his lips barely moving to produce the words. It was like his whole face was made of granite.

"What?" I felt a wave of panic sweep through me,

shifting my blood and turning me cold in a heartbeat. "What happened?"

"They found out about us." He folded his arms across his chest as if he needed to hold back his compulsion to punch something. *The wall? Me?* I wasn't sure. He had never been violent. Ever. But there were flecks of that potential radiating from his hazel irises.

"I don't understand," I insisted. My legs were shaking so badly that I had to sit down on the bed while I continued to look up at him, wishing I could penetrate through his steely exterior, reach right down to the heart I knew was buried in there—the one I loved and loved me back.

"Your big fucking mouth along with your big naked tits at the pool party last weekend cost me my job, Valley. What part of that do you not fucking understand?" He was frozen in place, still glaring at me, leaving those words hanging in the air like a tornado that continued to drill into me long after the sound had faded.

"I still don't understand. Who found out? Who fired you?"

"Bill did. The fucking priest, Valley. He basically said we're going to hell, and they can't have us building their church."

I was reeling. I just couldn't wrap my head around it. "How did he find out?"

"Remember that guy I was talking to at the Millers' pool party?"

I nodded.

"That was Art Vincent. He works with Phillip Miller, but his brother Allen is on the board at the church. He went to Bill and told him about the party, about you prancing around naked and basically said that we have questionable morals, and I shouldn't be part of this project."

It all seemed like a sick joke to me. My head was swirling, sending waves of nausea to attack my stomach. "I guess I don't understand why what we do in our private life has anything to do with their stupid church."

"We're in a small town, Valley. It's not our private life. You fucking displayed it for the whole world to see. You were drunk, naked, and out of control—and you had your boobs and lady parts hanging out all over the place. It's not funny. I'm probably going to have to move to even fucking work in this town again."

I froze with even more panic. I didn't realize I had gotten completely naked. *Surely he's just exaggerating?* As bad as him losing the church project was, because it was a huge source of income for us, I just kept thinking *but there will be other projects. It's just a setback.*

"What do you mean 'you're going to have to move?'" I glared right back at him. "Don't you mean 'we?'"

His face didn't soften even a tiny bit. "Well, I'm done with the lifestyle." As if he knew that would be the deal breaker.

"Oh, that's real fair. You get to fuck some hot chick—you got more action than I did during this whole thing—and before I even get a chance to have one good experience, you pull the plug?"

"I'm not the one who went blabbing about us swinging all over the neighborhood!"

"What are you talking about? It was one fucking pool party. I got a little drunk. Whatever. You could have taken me home if I was that much of an embarrassment to you."

"You told the Sullivans. And the Millers know too. The whole fucking neighborhood knows, Valley." I didn't know how it was possible, but his rage only seemed to be intensifying.

The weight of it crashed down on me like the ocean bears down on a deep sea diver. I was drowning from the pressure; my veins were about to explode. "So what are you going to do?"

"I don't know." His arms were still crossed over his chest. I wanted to be in those arms. I wanted my face to be pressed against his chest, feeling his warmth surround me, like it had this morning when we laid in bed spooning before he had to get up for work. I wanted things to just go back to where we were eight hours ago, the easy routine of waking up and starting our day together. The normalcy of it.

"Are you going to be able to forgive me?" I squeaked out. He'd built up a wall so high, I didn't even know if he could see me down here anymore. I felt invisible, my heart hidden from his, from the love I knew was there for me.

He shrugged as he continued to glare at me.

He shrugged.

Like he didn't know. Like he had forgotten who I was: *his wife, his rock, the mother of his children.*

I didn't say a word. I turned on my heel and left the room. Less than twenty minutes later, he slammed the front door behind him, and I heard his car start up in the driveway. I went to the window and watched him back out and drive away, his taillights glowing in the rapidly approaching dusk.

NEVER HAD MY BED FELT SO EMPTY. I TOSSED AND TURNED all night. That guy from the website I was supposed to meet kept texting me, even though I hadn't responded since before David came home from work. I did have a fleeting thought about going to meet him for a drink anyway—*Lord knows I needed a drink*—but A) I wasn't really in the mood anymore, and B) I looked like a complete wreck.

It had been a very long time since I'd cried this hard, like really blubbered, not since my father died a few years back. It's as if I had a whole reservoir of tears to drain. And it wasn't just a boo-hoo-hoo kind of cry. This was a full-body heaving, sinuses-filling-up-so-you-can't-breathe, chin-quivering, teeth-chattering kind of cry that soaks your clothes, sheets, and every scrap of material in sight. And I couldn't seem to stop.

I'd try to make myself eat. *Uncontrollable crying.*

I'd try to watch TV. *Uncontrollable crying.*

I tried to take a shower. *Uncontrollable crying.*

I was finally so miserable, I just forced myself to go to bed, even though it was only 9 PM. So much for making the most of my last day of Mommycation.

Shit, the kids. I had to decide what to do about the kids. I was supposed to drive over to David's parents' house to pick them up the next day. For all I knew, that is where he went. I fell asleep thinking that there was only one way to find out.

I LOOKED HIDEOUS, AND THERE WAS NO WAY MY MOTHER-in-law was going to let my appearance slide. She already thought I was too chubby and dressed too provocatively, but when she saw me with my uncombed hair thrown up into the messiest bun ever created, the dark purple circles underscoring my eyes, and my fuck-it-all wardrobe selections, she was really going to let me have it.

I showed up on her doorstep with a hoodie zipped up to my neck, even though it was well over 80 degrees outside. I didn't bother to remove my dark sunglasses either.

"Holy hell, Valley, what is wrong with you?" she questioned, recoiling at the sight of me. I'm sure in her eyes I looked like I'd been dredged up from the slimiest gutter.

David's car wasn't in the driveway, though I realized it was possible for him to have already left for the day. I knew better than to ask about him, though. If there was one thing I was not telling Joanna Archer, it was what happened between her son and me the day before.

"Are you sick?" she continued to press when I failed to answer. I wasn't sure if she could possibly contort her features into a nastier snarl of disapproval.

"Can I just get the kids and go home, please?" I tried to say it politely, but I wasn't in the mood to deal with her bullshit.

"Did someone die?" I loved how she didn't invite me into her home. Instead, she kept me on the porch with the door barely cracked open like I was some itinerant cult member asking her to join my church.

"Just, please, okay?" I attempted to appeal to the tiny semblance of a heart she had buried somewhere deep inside her, probably languishing from lack of use, right alongside her humility and sense of humor.

By some miracle, she acquiesced, throwing open the door and granting me access to their abode. I stepped inside, scanning the premises for my offspring. There was nothing more I wanted than to see their precious faces. I hoped I could keep it together when they finally appeared.

I heard their feet bounding down the staircase before they actually came into view. There was Aidan with his sharp features, just like his father's, and Aubrey, with her long, silky raven locks flying behind her. *Is it possible they grew an inch just since Joanna picked them up last week?* They looked taller. More mature. They ran into my arms, and I squeezed them tightly to my chest until Aidan protested, "Mom, you're hurting me*!" Oops, a bit too much squeezing*, I chided myself.

I thanked Joanna and told her to thank Hank for me too, though he seemed to be safely tucked away. It always seemed like he was in hiding whenever his wife was around. The only person he really seemed to enjoy hanging out with was David, now that I thought about it.

"Uh, you haven't seen—" I started to say "David," but then thought better of it right before his name slipped from my tongue.

"Seen whom?" she asked in her snooty voice.

"Aidan's soccer ball?" I lied. "It seems to be missing."

She shook her head. I thanked her again and ushered my children out to the car. Once we were all seat-belted in, I began to make the drive home to Sunview, wondering if my husband would be there when we returned.

There was no David when we returned home, but it was a weekday, so the kids just assumed he was at work. I took out my phone to text him, but then I decided against it. *I can be stubborn, but he walked out on me. Why should I be the one to make first contact?*

We had never gotten into a fight that lasted more than a few hours. I think we fought about Aubrey's name, and whether or not we would spend a holiday with his parents or mine. Sometimes I pouted when I didn't get as much sex as I wanted. But we had never, ever had a fight like this one. Never.

The kids seemed happy to be home and immediately retreated to their rooms. I was going to have to figure out something for us to do in the afternoon once I got cleaned up. I didn't think I could stay in this big house echoing with David's voice all day. I told them I was going to go shower, but first I went down to the basement.

The rooms were framed in for our project. We'd put

down plastic so the carpenters and contractors could come and go without tracking in, though I guessed it didn't matter if I was going to replace all the flooring. I hadn't decided yet.

What was I supposed to do with this space now if we weren't going to stay in the lifestyle? We didn't need three more bedrooms. How were we supposed to sell a house with 7 bedrooms and what looks like a kinky bed and breakfast in the basement?

We were waiting for the electrician and plumber to finish their jobs before the contractor sent in a drywall crew. That was all supposed to happen next week. Then I'd be hiring painters and someone to do the floors. I still hadn't decided—*new carpet in the bedrooms*, I supposed. *Tile everywhere else? Or hardwood. Probably tile. Easier to clean.* I was also putting up a new countertop in the bar area—granite. But I wondered if I should scale back and save that money in case—in case David asked for divorce?

I couldn't believe that word was even on my mind. We had vowed never, ever to even think of that word. It was not an option. We'd said from day one that we were a team, and there was nothing we couldn't overcome. *So why did he leave? Why did he break his promise to always work shit out?*

My phone buzzed just then with a text, and I felt my heart leap against my ribcage. I knew it was him without even looking. *He couldn't even call me; he just texted*, I thought as I scanned over his brief message. *I'm headed to Denver, checking out a potential project. I'll be in touch.*

That was it, so vague and cold. *Denver? What the hell?* That was hours away, even by plane. I shook my head, trying to keep the tears from stinging at my eyes again.

They were still swollen and irritated from all the crying I'd done the night before.

I proceeded upstairs to take a shower and try to put myself back together, but I was a puzzle missing the most integral piece. I told the kids we were going to go see that new superhero movie that came out earlier in the summer, and they seemed relatively excited as they scrambled around getting their shoes on.

"What about lunch, Mommy?" Aubrey asked with her beautiful green eyes shimmering.

Oh, fuck. I hadn't fed them all morning. I guess because I had forgotten to eat, I forgot about them too. *So add feeling like a worthless excuse for a Mom to my list of grievances,* I thought as I ushered them out the house and into the car. I promised them we'd grab lunch before heading over to the cinema at the Sunview Mall.

Finally, an hour later, we were nestled in our seats in the theater, and the previews had begun to roll. It had been a while since I'd taken the kids to the movies without David. It was usually something we did as a family. That thought tried to pry a tear from my eye, but I shook it off.

I glanced over at Aidan, who was stuffing his face with popcorn even though he barely ate his lunch. *Typical.* And then at Aubrey on my other side, whose face was painted with excitement. She reached over and grabbed my hand. I couldn't help but smile, feeling her smooth, tiny hand within mine.

As I sat there with my children and watched the story unfold on the screen, I realized that *they* were my projects, my *real* projects, my most *important* projects. Though I was excited to do something for myself for a change when

David and I decided to explore the lifestyle, I knew these little creatures sitting on either side of me were my true priorities. And no matter what happened between their father and me, they deserved the best of me.

It didn't hurt that the movie featured a female super-hero, and she was fucking incredible. She was, of course, beautiful. *It is Hollywood, after all.* But her beauty was surpassed by her strength and courage, and told the real story. I couldn't help but walk out of that theater feeling empowered. No matter what, I had this. I was going to keep it all together. I had no choice.

I TEXTED DAVID BACK WHEN WE GOT HOME FROM THE movies. *At least we were communicating, right?*

I asked him if he was planning to move to Denver. I didn't hear anything back right away.

The kids apparently had boundless energy to burn off after all the sugar they'd consumed that afternoon, so they took off like bullets to the backyard. I supposed I should get back to work on the media center project. And I realized I'd also failed to post my blog for the day.

I was on the fourth page of feedback that Emily had emailed me when David finally texted me back. *I'm just looking for other options*, he said.

It was hard for me to know if that meant he was only looking for work, or if he was looking for other romantic options too. He had never been good at communicating with words; he was much better in person. He always made me feel loved and appreciated, but he rarely had to demonstrate those feelings textually. I couldn't even remember the last time we'd spent more than a workday apart.

What am I supposed to tell the kids? I asked.

Tell them I had to go out of town on business, he answered.

When are you coming back?

When my business is completed.

I wanted to throw the phone across the room. Didn't he know how unfair he was being? I decided not to answer his last message and instead threw myself into my work.

Hours must have passed because I watched the shadows creep across the office until the golden radiance of late afternoon perched itself on my desk so brightly, I could barely see my computer screen. The kids had come back to roost as well. I could hear them zooming through the house as if they were running on fully charged batteries.

Weren't they supposed to crash after the sugar high wore off?

The doorbell rang, jolting me out of Mom mode for a moment. I wasn't expecting the contractors until tomorrow. When I opened the front door, I saw my gorgeous next-door neighbor standing there with a worried expression on his face.

"Hey, Erik! What a surprise! Come to borrow a cup of sugar?" I asked with a wink.

"Ah, hey, Valley. Sugar? No, I'm good." He chuckled a little bit, and his worried expression faded. I offered to let him inside, but he shook his head. "Oh, thanks, but Kyle's over, and um... Well..."

Now I was probably looking worried. I hoped the kids

hadn't been outside using my sex toys again. I nearly rolled my eyes at the thought.

"So, Kyle and I were in the backyard; your kids were… I guess playing tag and running through my yard, and—"

"Oh my God, Erik! I'm so sorry. They're really good kids and wouldn't knowingly trespass. It's just for the past couple months with the place vacant, they got a little lazy about sticking to our yard. Let me get them down here to apologize."

"Oh, no, really. That's not necessary. I couldn't care less if they run through the yard every day." He seemed surprised I would even suggest he was complaining about my little rugrats. "Kyle and I were kissing—all PG stuff. We were dressed, but the kids looked a little shocked. Maybe it was because they weren't expecting Kyle and me to be out there, or because we're two men kissing…I'm not sure. But I just wanted to let you know. And I'm really sorry." He looked genuinely remorseful, as if he had done something wrong, something really offensive.

His big blue puppy dog eyes were just so freaking adorable. *Why did he have to play for the other team?* I just laughed at the whole thing. "Oh, please, Erik. You have nothing to be sorry for. It's your yard, for Christ's sake!"

"Are you sure?" His eyebrow rose as his face washed with relief.

"Of course! I'll have a little talk with them, and really, they shouldn't be in your yard anyway."

"Thanks, Valley!"

"Of course! Have a great evening." Before he turned to leave, I decided to add, "By the way, if you were worried about it because you're gay, don't be. It's totally fine. I don't judge that sort of thing. Trust me, I know what it's like to be judged for being who you are. And it's not okay for people to do that. I'll make sure my kids know that's how I feel about it, too."

His lips spread into a grin. "Thanks, Valley, I really appreciate that."

I closed the door and called the kids into the kitchen. Sounding like a herd of elephants, they arrived a split second later, scrambling for the barstools and nearly knocking each other over in the process. I leaned over the counter, my eyes darting between theirs as their dark heads hung in anticipation of my words.

"When's Dad coming home?" Aidan asked before I got a word out of my mouth.

My face fell. I was hoping we could postpone that conversation, but I supposed it was inevitable. Better to get it over with. Like ripping off a band-aid. "Your dad had to fly to Denver unexpectedly for work," I announced.

Before we moved here, David had come to Sunview alone a few times to talk to some of the people heading up the projects he was taking on. The first projects he did were the movie theater and a large bank, and he met with the board and officers of the companies before finalizing the renderings.

But Sunview wasn't all that far away from where we lived, only a few hours by car, so he was back again late that night. The kids weren't used to their dad jetting off to far-away cities, and that fact was spread all over their faces as they looked up at me with huge eyes.

"Denver?" Aubrey asked, shaking her head.

"Yep. A new project in the works!" I assured them, even though I had no real clue what he was doing. I manually brightened my face so they wouldn't worry or think it was strange. Who would have guessed talking to them about our gay neighbor's PDA would be so much easier and less awkward?

"So, I guess you were in the neighbor's yard this afternoon?" I questioned, changing the subject.

They looked at each other as if trying to decide if they were going to own up to it. Then Aubrey slowly nodded her head. "Sorry, Mom," Aidan added.

"Oh, it's okay. He's not mad," I assured them. "It's just that he stopped by to say you might have seen him and his boyfriend kissing, and he wanted to make sure that wasn't a problem."

Aidan shrugged. "What kind of problem?"

My eyes pinned to my son's. He was such a miniature version of his father, right down to his gold-flecked hazel eyes. "A problem that you witnessed them kissing," I answered. "Not that he's gay. There's absolutely nothing wrong with that."

"What's 'gay' mean?" Aubrey asked.

"It's when boys like boys," Aidan answered before I had a chance to.

"It's when a person loves someone else who is the same gender as they are," I corrected him. "So men who love other men, and women who love other women."

"I love you, Mommy, and you're a girl, too," Aubrey said, her little face twisted in confusion.

"Not that kind of love." I smiled at her. "Romantic-type love. Like the type of love Mommies and Daddies have for each other."

"So it's like two Daddies or two Mommies?" Aubrey clarified.

"It could be, if they have kids. Or it might just be two

men or two women." I straightened to my full height as I considered how I could maximize this teachable moment. "Every family is different. Some families might have two adults and no kids. Some might have one adult and some kids. It doesn't matter how many people are in the family, only that they love each other."

"Like our family has a Mommy, a Daddy, a boy, and a girl," Aubrey listed, the concept starting to crystalize in her mind.

I tried not to wince at her statement, not knowing what was going to happen between her father and me. I nodded, biting my lip to hold back the tears stinging at my eyes.

"So it's fine for families to be different," I continued, "and it's okay for people to like different things. Some men love both men and women. Some women love men and other women too. It's like how you love pizza and macaroni and cheese. You don't have to choose which one you love more."

"Only when we go out to eat," Aidan retorted with a smirk. "You always make me choose one or the other."

I laughed. *So he took my analogy a little too literally.* "Any other questions?" I questioned, not wanting to overwhelm them with too much to think about.

"Yeah, what's for dinner?" my son asked. Then Aubrey put her little elbows on the table and joined in their chant of "Dinner! Dinner! Dinner!"

I KNOCKED TENTATIVELY ON JENNA'S DOOR, THINKING AT THE very last moment that perhaps she had a guy in there, and they were getting it on. I certainly wouldn't want to interrupt that, or deprive her from getting her freak on in any way, shape or form. But she answered just moments later, her beautiful smile spread across her cheeks all the way to her eyes, making me think she was genuinely happy to see me.

"Kids still gone?" I asked, and she nodded. "I just got mine back today." I sighed. "Guess my Mommycation is over."

"Mommycation?" she questioned, quirking a brow. "I think I like that term."

"Feel free to use it; it's not trademarked or anything." I stood there looking like a fool and forgetting why I even came over. *Oh, yeah, the media center.* No wonder she was staring at me with her face full of expectation. "I wanted to get your feedback on a couple of fabric selections," I finally said.

"Oh, okay, for the media center, you mean?" She was being so patient with me. I was never this much of a hot mess in front of people. I hated being this way, but the whole thing with David had really thrown me off-kilter.

I nodded and forced a smile as she swung the door open. "I can't stay very long. I left the kids at home alone for a few minutes."

"Oh? David's working late tonight?"

That was all it took. *Damn it!* The wall of tears that had been camping out behind my eyelids since this morning marched past the dam, flooding my eyes before I had the chance to stop them. *What the actual fuck?* I didn't cry in front of people. *This was unacceptable. Completely unacceptable!*

"Valley?" The look of shock on Jenna's face was so

animated, it looked like it belonged in a horror movie. It must have appeared as though an alien was clawing its way out of my eyes instead of just your garden variety, marital trouble type of tears.

I sobbed something unintelligible and had half a mind to turn and run back to my house, but the sweet lady just wrapped her arms around me and pulled me in for a hug. She walked me over to her sofa and gently pushed me down. It looked like she wasn't giving me a chance to escape. We were going to do the girly thing and talk about it. *Damn it.* I hated the girly thing.

"What's going on?" she asked, stroking my back and trying to comfort me. As the mother of twin girls, I had a feeling this was a role she was pretty used to. When Aubrey was upset, I basically treated her the same way as Aidan. I told her, "Chin up! You've got this, girl!" I didn't have the whole nurturing, let-'em-cry-it-out gene, nor did my mother use that tactic with me when I was growing up.

"David left. We got into a huge fight about our—lifestyle," I blubbered, letting the word come out before I could stop it. Well, Nina and Jayne already knew. Jenna probably did too. The whole fucking neighborhood did, apparently.

Jenna nodded as if she wasn't the least bit surprised. She patted my back and waited for me to reveal more.

"I don't know if he's coming back. I don't know if our marriage is over or what," I sobbed, wiping my tears on the tissue she handed me. She was armed and ready, definitely not a newb to the fine art of consolation. Plus, I realized, she had just gone through her own divorce. She was no stranger to marital strife either—or broken relationships, for that matter.

"He'll be back." Her voice was full of confidence. "He just needs time to process everything. You know how men are. They can't talk shit out like we can."

I softly chuckled in spite of the tears still streaming down my cheeks. "He's in Denver looking for a new job."

Her face morphed into shock again. "Denver? He lost his job?" She looked absolutely incredulous.

I nodded. "He was working on a big project for a church. Word got around that we're swingers, and they fired him."

"Oh my god, Valley, that's horrible!" She straightened up a little, removing her hand from my back. "He's probably mad about that, sweetie, not mad at you."

I shook my head as I expelled a deep breath from my lungs. "No, he blames me. He blames me for being so indiscreet—not to mention drunk—at the Miller's pool party last weekend. Some people gossiped, and it got back to the church board."

"Wow." She was stunned. I could tell she was wrestling with the right words to comfort me and was coming up short on finding them. I certainly couldn't blame her for that.

I stood to leave. "I'm sorry. I shouldn't have even said anything. Hell, if Emily finds out, I'll probably get kicked off the media center project."

She laughed. "Would that be such a bad thing?"

I joined her, letting a little mirth out in spite of my pain. "No, probably not." I ran my fingers through my hair and tried to settle down my tears, knowing I needed to get back home to the kids. I didn't want them to see me like this.

She stood up too and gave me another hug. "I'm sure you guys will work things out."

"Thanks, Jenna. I hope you're right."

As soon as I shut her front door, I realized we never talked about the media center project. *Oh, well.* I needed the girl talk a lot more than I needed help preparing for Emily Walter's scrutiny. I mean that was a given.

Walking back to my house, I looked at it from afar and thought about how sad it was that I wouldn't get to throw my end-of-summer swinger bash. Especially after all the work I'd put into the basement, work that wasn't even done, but still had to be paid for. I thought about the fact that I never really got to have a successful experience, other than making out and the girl-on-girl stuff with Hailey. I couldn't believe we'd tried for almost two months and were still waiting for the perfect full-swap experience.

Then it dawned on me that I didn't need David. I could throw my own party. I didn't know if I would actually play; that certainly depended on him and what he decided about our future. But I didn't see why I couldn't play hostess with the mostest and invite all of our swinger friends over to celebrate our perfect swinger lair. I decided to march right home, get on the website, set a date and send out the invites.

I needed a distraction from this horrible sadness that was sitting in the pit of my stomach like a bomb about to go off. And now I had a party to plan.

❧ 14 ❧

I finished writing the check to the contractor and then walked him to the door. Drywalling was to start the next day, and the new appliances would start arriving any time. I ordered curtains, chose tile and carpet, and hired the painters. I was all over this project, even without David's help.

We had talked on the phone now twice. He said he had some good news to share with me, but I didn't want to hear that we were moving. I didn't want to go to Denver. I loved the warm climate in Sunview and wasn't sure I could handle snow for most of the year.

He didn't come home right away, either. He said he was going to visit his brother in Minnesota for a guy's camping and fishing trip. I just rolled my eyes at that.

David's brother Gabe hadn't been home to visit his parents in three years because of a falling out he'd had with his mother. I couldn't really blame him; Joanna was impossible to please. He'd been divorced almost the whole time I'd known him and was now living the bachelor life up north, where he'd moved because his ex-wife was from there and she wanted to be near her parents.

I was worried about him making the bachelor life seem a little too glamorous. He and his ex were on good terms and had joint custody, and I thought he might try to paint a pretty rosy picture of how things could be for David if he wanted to venture down that path.

Years ago, Gabe had tried to end our engagement because he felt strongly David should play the field a little longer before settling down. Apparently, Gabe hadn't sowed enough wild oats in his youth, and naturally, he regretted it. At six years older than David, he thought he knew everything. His marriage only lasted a few years, so what did that say about him?

Gabe was a jerk, just like his mom. He'd never get remarried because no woman in her right mind would be stupid enough to get involved with him.

I told the kids their dad wouldn't be home for another week and was met with sighs and groans. "Why can't I go on the camping and fishing trip too?" Aidan complained. "I'm a guy."

I guess I'd made the mistake of saying it was a "guy's trip." Oops.

Then Aubrey started in, "I've always wanted to go fishing. How come Daddy has never taken *me* fishing?"

I made a mental note to invest in earplugs. *How did Aubrey's voice suddenly develop that perfect whining pitch that could practically burst your eardrums?*

"Look, guys, I'm sorry. Let's go do something fun this weekend, okay? There's a new water park over in Easton we could check out. What do you say?"

"Water park? Yeah!" Aidan shouted, making a little fist pump in the air.

"That might be fun," Aubrey said; she was always more skeptical than her brother.

"Can I invite Van and Shane to come?" Aidan asked.

"Maybe," I answered. "I'm sending you guys over there tonight while I go to the PTA meeting, so we can ask."

"Eww, I have to go hang out with the boys?!" Aubrey groaned.

"It's just for a couple hours. Sorry, sweetie, but Ms. Watson has to go to the meeting too. You want your school to have a new media center, right?"

"Yeah, but I don't want to hang out with boys," she said firmly.

"You will someday," I teased her.

I TRIED MY HARDEST NOT TO BE LATE TO THE MEETING AT school, but Posey held me up with some chit-chat when I dropped off the kids. She's obviously head over heels in love and wants to tell everyone about it.

I couldn't let on that David and I are having issues, obviously, so I tried to be polite. She did promise Aubrey that they would bake cookies, and that seemed to put a smile on her little face, so I was glad about that. *They miss their dad. I miss him too.*

Naturally, Emily Walters was perched on her throne, er, behind her podium ready to call the meeting to order when I snuck in. Every fucking eye in the joint moved at warp speed to have a look at me, even though I was dressed conservatively in white capris and a one-shoulder black top. I felt the stares continue to bore into me, accompanied by little snickers of laughter and gossip as I took my seat over to the side.

Jenna tried to flash me a sympathetic smile, but the teacher next to her touched her arm and leaned to whisper something in her ear while pinning her eyes right to mine. *Fucking bitch*. I knew they were talking about me.

The meeting proceeded with a lot of unnecessary bullshit until Emily called me up to the podium to share my slideshow of designs for the new space. As I clicked through them, I could tell no one was paying any attention to my voice or my presentation. Their eyes were glued to me, my body. Maybe it was the way the very tops of my breasts pushed up from my blouse, or the way the white stretchy denim fabric hugged the curves of my hips.

I had no idea why all these judgy bitches were staring at me when we were here to discuss the media center project, but I was THIS CLOSE to giving them all a fucking piece of my mind when Emily joined me at the podium, putting her arm around me.

When her skin met mine, I almost jumped to the ceiling. I was certainly not expecting her to touch me, and I would have thought her skin would feel cold, clammy and lizard-like. Instead, she was warm. Tender even. Not just temperature, but her voice too.

"Valley has worked really hard to put all this together for us, and she's done an amazing job. Let's all give her a round of applause for the incredible design she's come up with," Emily said, kicking off the applause with the loudest clapping I had ever heard.

The ladies in the audience reluctantly followed her lead, clapping their hands together slowly at first, then picking up speed. I smiled smugly and took my seat, thinking how lucky they were not to be on the receiving end of the can of whoop-ass I was about to unleash on them.

After the meeting ended and everyone began to filter from the room, Emily called out my name. I whipped around, thinking she had more instructions for me to prepare for the next meeting. I was surprised to see a warm smile affixed to her face. I wasn't sure her lips could even bend that way. I returned to where she was standing, and it was clear she wanted to speak, but she seemed to be waiting for everyone else to leave first.

"What is it?" I finally asked when no one else remained.

"I heard what happened with your husband," she said without even a trace of judgment on her face.

"What do you mean?" My eyes darted between hers as I waited for her to explain herself. Maybe I was mistaking her gloating for warmth.

"I heard your husband lost his contract with the Catholic church because you're swingers," she clarified, lifting her glasses off her face, folding them and tucking them into a case in her purse.

Shit. Word really did get around. I guessed this was what we deserved for trying to swing in such a small town. When we started getting involved, and I told David I didn't care what people thought, I was only thinking about myself. I guess I should have been more worried about how people perceived him.

I was sure now that the sparkle dancing in Emily's eyes was one of triumph, as though she'd finally broken me and was now basking in her glory. I wasn't expecting what she said next.

"It's hard for me to tell you this..." She glanced around to make absolute certain no one would hear her next words. The room was as silent as a church, *pardon the pun.* "But Gary and I are in the lifestyle too."

You probably could have knocked me over with a feather.

Cobweb Coochy was a SWINGER?! Are you fucking kidding me?

She laid her hand on my arm. "Oh, don't look so surprised!" She laughed, spreading a soft rose-colored blush across her usually sallow cheeks. "You know what they say about 'a lady in the streets and a freak in the sheets!'"

I was still speechless. *And I am not the type to be rendered speechless by anything or anyone.* I waited for the dust to settle from her bomb before finally asking, "Why are you telling me this?"

She cleared her throat. "I feel really bad about what happened to you. And though I don't think there's any kind of official swinger code to this effect, I do know we look out for each other. I want to help make things right."

"What do you mean?" My heart was now thundering against my chest so hard I thought it might crack my ribs.

"My husband Gary is the president of the board for Sunview Public Schools, not sure if you were aware."

Of course I was aware. That's what made them being swingers even more unbelievable. How they were able to go undercover in this small community was truly incredible. But I still wasn't following how that could help me or David.

"They're getting ready to put out a bid request for the new high school set to open in a few years. They were thinking of one of the bigger firms from the city, but I know they'd much prefer a local architect take it on. We just didn't think there was anyone here in town with that much commercial or industrial experience."

My eyes grew so wide, I'm sure it looked as though they might pop right out of my head. "So you're saying you want to work with David?"

"It's a definite possibility." She reached into her pocket and pulled out a business card. "Just have him set up an appointment with Gary. He knows what's going on, and he wants to help too."

I was still reeling from this news, but I took both of her hands into mine and pumped them up and down like she'd just told me I won the lottery. "Thank you so much, Emily. I am so sorry I misjudged you. You might have just saved my marriage!"

She gave me a kiss on the cheek as she hugged me tightly to her chest. "I'm glad I could help.

I WAS PACKING THE KIDS' THINGS FOR OUR WATERPARK getaway when I heard a car pull into the driveway. I ran into the office and glanced out the window at the front of the house because I knew it was him. It was David, returning from his trip a few days earlier than I expected him.

I swear my heart skipped a beat as he stepped out of the car and I got a look at him. He was still the tall, handsome man I'd married with thick brown hair, the kind of hair that made other men jealous, a straight nose, perfect teeth and a strong jaw. Only the latter was covered in hair as though he hadn't thought to take a razor with him.

Before he could make it up the steps, I heard the kids slam the door and run out to greet him. I couldn't see their reunion, but I could hear it. Aubrey was squealing so loudly, I thought she might burst the glass in the windows. I walked to the foyer and peered out the window as my husband bent to gather his children into his arms. They were so happy to see him, and it looked like he had missed them every bit as much as they'd missed him.

They walked inside hand in hand, leaving his suitcase in the driveway until our adorable, thoughtful son realized and went back to collect it. I watched him lug it up the stairs, taking every bit of his ten-year-old strength. I felt tears stinging at my eyes again when I'd managed not to cry for the past couple of days. Ever since Emily had given me that business card, I'd just been filled with hope that we would be able to fix everything I'd broken.

David's eyes pierced into me as soon as the door shut behind him. I glanced down and saw that Aubrey was watching us, waiting for us to embrace. He didn't hesitate, but pulled me into his arms immediately. His clean, manly scent filled my senses as he squeezed me to his chest with his arms wrapped tightly around me. I opened my eyes and saw the kids had vanished, almost like they knew we needed privacy.

"Let's go talk," he said, tugging my hand toward the bedroom.

I followed him, wondering for a moment if his hug in the foyer was meant to appease the children and not for me. Butterflies danced in my stomach as I prepared myself for what he might say about his travels and any decisions he had come to along the way.

When we were inside the room, he shut the door and turned to face me. His features were neutral, and it was impossible for me to tell what he was planning to say. His eyes traveled up and down my body, making me a little self-conscious and wishing I'd made more of an effort. I was just wearing a simple tank top and shorts for the water park, nothing special.

"I missed you," he finally blurted out, and I spotted a tear glistening in the corner of his eyes. If there was one person on the planet who was less likely to cry than I was, it was my husband. He was not a crier, never had been. I hadn't seen him shed a tear since...well, I didn't even remember when the last time was.

"I missed you too, David, but—" He wasn't off the hook. He'd left me for over a week and barely told me what was going on. He'd hurt me. Even though I'd made my share of mistakes, I certainly never set out to deliberately hurt him, and if he thought he could just waltz back in here and pretend like nothing was wrong, well, he had another thing coming.

"Valley, please," he said, sighing. His eyes grazed mine again before they caressed my curves. I knew that look. It was desire. He wanted me.

"The basement is almost done," I told him. "And I'm throwing a party in August. Just so you know."

"Okay," he answered, not seeming to protest. "How do you feel about moving?" he asked. "The party could be our going away party."

I shook my head as I folded my arms across my chest.

"I don't want to move again," I insisted. "I like it here. I've made friends. The kids have made friends."

"You've made friends?" he scoffed. "Like who?"

"All our lifestyle friends. Plus Jenna, Posey, and Emily Walters," I answered, glaring at him. How dare he act like I didn't have any friends. *He's the one who insisted I make them and try to fit in here in the first place!*

"Emily Walters? Isn't that the PTA chick? I thought you hated her."

"She turned out to be different than I thought," I explained, more than happy to defend her after all she'd done for me.

He looked confused, but his expression quickly changed to one of resolution. "It doesn't matter. We can't stay here. There's not enough work here. I've got a new project in Denver, and as a matter of fact, I have to fly back there on Monday to get started."

I shook my head again. "Thanks for letting me in on the whole planning process." I firmed my stance and stared at him. "

"You cost me that job with the church," he said.

Oh, I wondered how long it would take for that to come up. "David, I want to stay here. In Sunview with my friends. With our friends. With our kids' friends. And the lifestyle stuff. I don't want to move again. We haven't even been here a full year yet!"

His hand flew up to press against his temple, as if I was giving him a vicious headache for not jumping on his Denver bandwagon. "I don't think you understand, Valley. I don't have work here. That church project was the only one I had. There aren't any big projects to keep me here right now. That's why I had to leave—to find work. I have to take care of my family."

I turned on my heel.

"Where are you going?" he demanded.

I grabbed Gary Walter's business card off the dresser behind me and thrust it into David's hand. He turned it over and read it, then glanced up at me with questioning eyes.

"They want you to design the new high school," I told him. "Gary is Emily Walter's husband. They're in the lifestyle too, and they want to help us. Just set up an appointment with him and see if you can work something out."

"She told you that?" he confirmed, looking down at the card again.

I nodded. "This is a good community, David. I love our neighbors; I love the school. I don't love living so close to your parents, but I do love them being able to watch the kids." I couldn't help but smirk at that last admission. "I don't want to leave."

"Do you still love me?" he asked, his hazel eyes locking with mine and the expression on his face transforming into one of hope.

"Yes, David, I still love you."

And just like that, I was back in his arms. Right where I belonged.

It's so nice when you complete a project and can sit back and enjoy the fruits of your labor. I planned to enjoy all sorts of fruits...of the phallic variety...at the party we were hosting. The kids were off at my in-laws' house, so we had the whole weekend together and with friends.

I looked around the space that we created. The accent wall at the back of the house where the French doors leading to the patio was a deep, rich crimson, and the rest of the walls were a cool gray. The bedrooms were done in jewel tones: one in amethyst, one in emerald, and one in a striking jade, which was my favorite. The linens were luxurious and plush, with high thread-count sheets and the duvet covers over the fluffy down comforters were silky smooth. I knew for a fact that they felt amazing against the skin because David and I had actually christened each room this week, one per night leading up to the party. Then I washed all the sheets and tidied up the rooms so they'd be perfect for our guests.

"The wine is chilling," David called from the mini kitchen. Though it was small compared to our kitchen upstairs, it was as large as the main kitchen in many homes.

The bar was especially long, accommodating five barstools, and its sleek granite countertop matched the gray walls perfectly. The fixtures were all brushed nickel, and the bathroom matched. With the stainless steel refrigerator, mini stove, dishwasher and sink, everything looked clean and modern.

"And the keg?" I asked him.

"On the patio, ready to go," he confirmed.

Any minute, the caterer would be arriving with a tasty selection of hors d'oeuvres. The house parties David and I had been to before were usually potluck, and while they had a nice, homey feel to them, I wanted ours to be a step up. I didn't know how often David would allow me to host extravagant soirees down here, so I figured I better make this one count. He hadn't complained, but then again, he hadn't seen all the final credit card bills either. *wink*

"I'm going upstairs to change," I warned him, and he turned to me and nodded. I turned to go, but he stopped me by calling out my name. "What?"

"Come here for a minute," he requested, and I obliged.

"What, darling?"

He lifted his hand to my face where he traced from my cheekbone down to my chin with his fingertips. I was just wearing a tank top with no bra and a pair of short, terrycloth shorts. I hadn't done my makeup yet and my hair was piled on top of my head. I was pretty much a mess. I couldn't wait to undergo my transformation into hot, sexy Valley. The way his eyes pierced into me made me feel almost naked, but his lips remained still, unspeaking. His eyes were relaying a message; it was up to me to interpret it.

No words were needed as he brushed his thumb over my lips and then replaced it with his mouth, which was so soft and gentle, it felt like a whisper against my sensitive skin. "David," I gasped, thinking if he kept that up, I wouldn't be making it upstairs to get ready any time soon.

"Shhhh," he whispered against my lips. His eyes fluttered open and he pulled back ever so slightly so he could see my face.

"David, I'm a mess. Let me go get changed…"

"No," he protested, his eyes roaming over my face again, taking in my smooth, unadorned skin and my bare eyes and lips. "You don't need all that makeup and those sexy clothes, Valley. You're absolutely stunning without all of that."

My heart fluttered as I absorbed his words. I would never leave the house like this. I couldn't stand being out in public without my face on, without an "outfit," something that accentuated my curvy body. No one ever saw me as David did at this moment: my pure, raw self.

"Not that you don't look great when you get all dolled up," he explained, "but I prefer you like this. Just Valley. My beautiful, sensual, vibrant Valley."

His lovely sentiments resonated through me like a bell; so clear and bright, the sound wrapped around me like an embrace. And I followed suit, folding my arms around his waist, pulling myself to him until our bodies pressed together with not even a molecule of air between us.

"I love you, David," I whispered against his neck, and then he lifted my chin again to seal his lips over mine.

THE PARTY WAS IN FULL SWING BY NINE O'CLOCK. I'D invited nearly all the couples we'd met so far in the lifestyle, plus a few more that Ed and Shawna recommended. Our space looked a lot different with forty people in it, and it was much louder than I had anticipated. So far, it looked like an upscale cocktail party; everyone was roaming around with drinks in their hands, mingling and happily munching on the gourmet hors d'oeuvres.

I spotted a couple in the corner not really interacting with anyone. I knew their profile on the site, and they were friends with Ed and Shawna, but I had never been properly introduced. No time like the present, I thought as I headed over their way. "Hi again, having fun?"

"Hey, Valley," the man replied, an uneasy smile working its way across his face. "My wife is a little overwhelmed by crowds."

She shot him a dagger-filled look, then playfully smacked him on the arm. "Sorry, Valley, Ryan needs more beer, I think." She winked at me and then smacked her hubby again for good measure.

"Well, we can certainly arrange that. There's a keg out on the patio. Have you guys seen the hot tub yet?"

Her eyes lit up. "It's Melanie, right?" I confirmed as I looked her up and down. Sometimes I knew couples better from their screen names on the site than their actual first names. I was pretty sure Ryan and Melanie were *funshycouple32*. I understood the "shy" part of their username now.

She nodded at me, her lips barely curving into a smile. She was a bit hesitant, but she had no reason to be. She was absolutely stunning, with a curvy, buxom figure, long brown hair that curled around her shoulders seductively and pretty blue eyes. Her husband was good looking too, with thick sandy brown hair, broad shoulders and light hazel eyes. And tall. *Damn.* He had to be every bit of 6'4" I noticed as he stood up.

"Follow me!" I motioned toward the patio door, then scanned the room for David. He wasn't in sight, so I assumed he was already outside. When we stepped out onto the patio, there were people milling about, but no one was in the hot tub yet. Ryan made his way over to the keg and filled up a cup before rejoining Melanie and me. I found David talking to Ed and Shawna over by the grill.

"Hey, guys!" I said, greeting our friends with kisses on each of the cheeks. "Mind if I borrow David for a moment? I want to introduce him to Ryan and Melanie."

"He's all yours!" Shawna winked at me, then reached down to give David's ass a squeeze in his loose-fitting khaki shorts.

I pulled David over to where Ryan and Melanie were still standing on the other side of the hot tub. The patio light was falling just perfectly to illuminate her, like she was standing in a spotlight. I scanned David's face as his eyes roamed up and down her body. I could already tell he was taken with her. Devious thoughts began to form in my mind, but I knew they weren't ready yet.

"I think I'm going to refill my drink," Melanie announced after I made the introductions.

"Oh, allow me to accompany you to the bar," David piped up. I loved it when my plans fell into place!

Ryan and I stood in silence for just a moment before he spoke. "Your house is amazing. Did you guys build it?"

I shook my head. "No, but we did just redesign this space here in our basement."

"It turned out great! I was just thinking it was the perfect place for one of these parties!"

"That was the idea," I replied, winking at him. There was just a short beat of awkward silence before I followed it up with, "Are you guys new to the lifestyle?"

He nodded. "Pretty new. We started last New Year's Eve at Ed and Shawna's party. We didn't know what we were getting ourselves into, that's for sure. But we're enjoying it so far. Melanie is pretty shy, and I'm not exactly forward myself."

"Yeah, I bet it's hard for shy people," I agreed. "I'm not shy. In case you didn't notice." I laughed, hoping to make him feel more comfortable. I wasn't going to bite—not unless he was into that sort of thing. In that case, it could certainly be arranged.

He turned toward me, squaring his body up with mine. "I really like that about you, Valley," he said as though he was trying out my name on his tongue. His suggestive tone made me think he might want to try other things out with his tongue as well.

"I hope that's not all you like about me." I gave him a sultry smile.

"Oh, I would say that is one of many," he answered, "but you know, I'm just getting to know you. So there is plenty of...uncharted territory."

I liked the way his voice dropped into a gravelly baritone on the last two words. "Have you guys gotten to play much?"

He shook his head. "We haven't at all...yet. I guess you could say we're looking for the right couple."

I nodded with a devious glint in my eyes. "I know exactly what you mean."

David and Melanie returned, each with a mixed drink. They were both purple. I raised my eyebrow and glanced over at David. "New concoction?"

He nodded. "I call it Purple Paradise," he answered with a wink. "Pretty good, huh, Melanie?"

She murmured in agreement as she took another sip.

"Almost like your username on the website, *ProjectParadise*," Ryan noted, his eyes dancing with wicked thoughts. He was turning out to be even more alluring than I'd originally thought. "So, how do you know when your project has been completed?"

I locked my eyes onto his as I quipped in my sultriest voice, "I'll let you know later tonight..." Melanie giggled as if she perfectly understood my innuendo. I was beginning to like these two...a lot.

"Oh, excuse me for a minute, guys. We'll be right back." I grabbed David and steered him in the direction of the couple who had just arrived. I barely recognized her with her auburn hair straightened and without the librarian glasses perched on her nose. "Emily!" I shouted, and she whipped her head in my direction.

We moved closer to each other, ending our journey in a warm embrace. "I'm so glad you made it!"

She pulled back and smiled at me. "I wouldn't have missed it for the world! I'm so glad you guys are staying!"

I had never seen her outside of her frumpy mom

uniform, but tonight she was wearing a tiny little ruffled skirt and an off-the shoulder cropped top that showed her perfect abs and tight little body off to perfection. *Who knew she was hiding that under those ugly clothes?!* "Emily, you look fucking amazing!" I gasped.

"Thanks!" She twirled around, the skirt lifting into the air and showing off her slim, shapely legs.

I turned to her husband. "Can I give you a hug?! I'm just so thrilled we were able to work everything out."

"You can give me more than a hug!" he answered, pulling me in for a tight bear squeeze and a kiss on the lips that made that perfect smacking sound.

"We're lucky to have you on this project. The board loved your portfolio, David. Just think, your son Aidan and our daughter Ava will be the first class to start at the new high school!" Emily pointed out.

"And that means we get to stay in Sunview!" I cheered. "I'm so happy and relieved."

"Which means plenty more parties in this space, right?" Gary confirmed as he grabbed my hand. "You better give me the grand tour, my dear!"

I squeezed his arm and nodded. "That can be arranged!"

IT'S AMAZING WHAT TWO HOURS, A HOT TUB AND SOME alcohol can do to a crowd of swingers. I watched the conversations become laced with increasingly overt innuendo and hands and lips begin to more freely express themselves. The bedroom doors opened and closed. Muffled screams failed to be blocked out, even with the soundproofing we'd had installed. The music got a little louder. The keg was being drained, along with other... ahem...appendages. Empty wine bottles and cups were left in various locations. I had smartly hired a cleaning crew to come in the next day.

I found Ryan and Melanie soaking in the hot tub around midnight. David asked if we could join them. Surprisingly, they were the only people in the tub.

"Where did everyone go?" Melanie asked as I submerged myself into the bubbling water.

"I think they're all fucking," I replied, with perhaps a hint of wistfulness in my voice.

"Lucky bastards!" Ryan exclaimed as he wrapped his arm around me. He pulled me toward him, and I could smell beer on his breath, only faintly though, thank goodness. He brushed his lips against mine as if he was testing my response.

My answer was to open my mouth, tilt my head back and allow him full access. I swallowed his moan as it became clear he wasn't going to get much resistance out of me.

I'd had my eyes on him all night. He'd been my target from the moment he walked through the door, and I had the feeling David felt the same way about Melanie as he began to devour her with just as much passion.

I might have been a little too anxious when I felt Ryan's stiff cock pressing against me as I straddled him. All I could think about was how this was finally going to happen—tonight—and how long I had waited for this. He was teasing the hell out of my nipples, and when he slid his hand down to touch the smooth, bare skin of my pussy, I wasn't sure how much longer I could wait.

Maybe I felt an increased sense of urgency because I was afraid something would happen to keep us from going all the way. I felt like I was in high school again, sneaking around behind our parents' backs, trying to do the deed before anyone figured out we were missing.

Slow down, I kept chiding myself. *This isn't a race.*

From the sounds David and Melanie were making, though, it seemed like they were just as ready as I was. I broke away from Ryan's lips, and it was as if David's radar went off. Our eyes met over the steamy water and he nodded before I had a chance to ask. "Let's go inside," I whispered in Ryan's ear, and I swear his cock twitched against my stomach in response.

I climbed out and handed our guests and David a towel before taking one for myself. I was naked long enough for most of the water to evaporate anyway, but not the devoted stares of everyone within gawking distance.

"God damn, Valley!" Ed yelled across the yard. "Those are some fucking fine tits you got there, woman!"

"I'll drink to that!" Shawna echoed his enthusiasm, lifting her cup of Purple Paradise David had mixed for her into the air. "To Valley!" she shouted.

"To Valley and David!" came the cheer lifted up from the crowd who had gathered outside.

I tempered my excitement for what was about to happen with the realization that something could still go awry, even at this last moment. Someone could get cold feet; Mother Nature could cock-block us...but just seeing the grins on all my friends' faces and hearing their cheering voices lifted up in unison was enough.

I'd done it. I'd thrown the perfect swinger party, and

I'd found a place where I could be myself—and be adored for it.

I glanced over at Ryan, whose towel was doing nothing to conceal his giant boner—*a boner meant for me*, I thought with a salacious smirk.

He bit his lip as if he couldn't wait to see what I did next. I curled my index finger and beckoned him to follow me, and the four of us headed inside the house to my favorite room, the jade one. It was unoccupied, and the candles I'd lit at the beginning of the night were still flickering, filling the room with a sensual jasmine and gardenia scent.

"This room is absolutely gorgeous," Melanie gasped, though I wasn't sure how she could fully appreciate it without the lights on.

"Not as gorgeous as you are," David told her, wrapping his arms around her and drawing her close to his body.

Ryan whipped me around to face him, then let his towel drop to the floor so his bare skin, still warm and damp from the hot tub, pressed into mine. He pulled the ponytail holder that secured my long, black hair into a bun on top of my head so that my tresses came tumbling down around my shoulders. Then he peeled away the towel I'd wrapped around myself for our short walk inside.

I ran my fingers down his rippled chest and abdomen, then dropped to my knees on the floor. I was glad I sprang for the expensive carpet, because it felt soft against my bare knees, and I knew I was in no danger of getting rugburn. I looked up at him, and in the candlelight, his eyes were dark, needy and lustful.

I wrapped my fingers around his cock at the base and

then ever so lightly ran the tip of my tongue up his shaft, feeling him shudder underneath my taste buds. "Did you like that?" I asked teasingly, though I knew perfectly well that he did.

"More please," was all he could manage as his eyes rolled back in his head. I looked over and saw that David had already spread Melanie out on the bed was performing a similarly teasing maneuver to her pussy.

Before he could take another breath, I engulfed the entirety of his thick rod in my mouth, taking him all the way to the back of my throat until I nearly gagged. That breath got caught in his mouth, and he nearly choked on it. Finally, after I managed to stroke my lips back and forth a few times, he let out a, "God damn, Valley...."

His hands threaded through my hair as he continued to pump in and out of my mouth. I slowed down, not wanting him to come yet. All I wanted was that cock inside of me. Now that it had filled up my throat, I could only imagine how it would feel filling my pussy. I wrapped my lips around him and went from base to tip one time, just holding him there to swirl my tongue around his crown. His thighs began to tremble, and I knew how close he must be, how hard he was working to hold back.

"I'm going to blow it right in your mouth if you don't stop," he said, confirming my suspicions.

I nodded with a wicked grin spreading my lips. Just then, Melanie's voice shattered the silence as a climax ripped through her, and she writhed under my husband's tongue.

"I should probably give you an orgasm before I fuck

you," Ryan said, tilting my face back to look at him. He grabbed my arm and pulled me up to standing.

I loved how tall he was. Even at 5'8", I just did come up to his shoulders. He was just a positively delicious piece of man meat. It would have been nice to get a taste of his oral skills (*pun intended*), but just looking at that glorious rock-hard cock jutting out at me, my body only wanted one thing, and it was painfully clear what that one thing was. The pressure had built up so intensely in my core, I thought I might come just from having him between my legs.

"No, I want your cock inside me, now," I corrected him, grabbing onto his tool and brushing it against my clit as I shuddered with need. "Grab a condom and meet me over there." I pointed to the bed next to his wife, who was in the process of coming down from her climax. David had worked his way up her body with a trail of kisses but had gotten distracted somewhere around her right nipple.

Ryan did as directed and started rolling the condom down his shaft as he walked back to the bed. I shivered with the excitement that was blooming throughout my body. It seemed like this was finally going to happen after waiting for *months*. He climbed on top of me, positioned himself between my legs and pressed his lips to mine. The heat from his mouth radiated throughout my body, stealing my breath and making my clit throb with anticipation.

"Are you ready for me?" he murmured, though I'm sure he knew the answer from the way my body quivered beneath him. He reached between us, gliding his hand down to my pussy.

I gasped as his finger slid inside me. "Fuck, Valley!" he

groaned against my cheek. "You're so fucking wet."

"I want you," I reiterated, bucking against him, hoping to catch the tip of his cock with my pussy lips.

He didn't say another word, but instead guided his cock toward me until the crown rested upon my swollen clit. The walls of my pussy spasmed just then, preparing to milk the cum from his balls. I hadn't been this close to the edge of an orgasm for so long...if ever. I felt like I might come unhinged if he didn't fill me with his throbbing manhood in the next second. He pressed against me as I grabbed his ass cheeks, pulling him closer and guiding him inside me inch by glorious inch, reaching to the very depth of me until I let out a sharp moan. *Fuuuuuuck*. It felt so amazing.

"Jesus, you're so tight," he grunted as he caught his breath and began to stroke inside me. I noticed out of the corner of my eye that David had completed his kissing circuit and had gone to retrieve a condom.

I felt suspended in an ethereal state, right on the brink, but not falling off. Watching David mount Melanie and prepare himself for entering her kept me balanced there, waiting. Ryan buried his face in my neck, where he was letting out short, deep growls as he tried to keep a steady rhythm, resisting the temptation to go too fast. The slow pace was killing me; all I needed were a few fast, deep thrusts, and I knew I would explode around him.

As David slid into Melanie and she wrapped her legs around his hips, his eyes locked onto mine. When I saw his lips curl up into a smile, my own mouth mirrored his. He reached for my hand, which had been on Ryan's back, trying to push him deeper inside me as I thrusted my pelvis up to match each of his strokes.

Once my hand was enclosed in my husband's, my eyes snapped shut, and I felt myself become carried away by the sensations, the warmth of David's hand, the heat of Ryan's breath against my neck, the sounds of Melanie's moans as David pushed into her, the feel of Ryan's throbbing cock reaching to the depths of me.

The waves cascaded over me like nothing I had ever felt before, spurred on by the rhythmic motion of four bodies, all dancing the same steps in and out, in and out. Engulfed by the purple bliss, I rode the highest wave until it spit my body back out on the shore, full and satiated.

Everyone had gone home, and we turned our eyes away from the mess as we ventured back out onto the patio. The stars were fading into a heather blue as the first rosy fingers of dawn began to stretch their way past the horizon. I couldn't believe we partied all night. I couldn't believe I finally had another man. I couldn't believe it had all gone so perfectly!

"Well?" David asked, eyeing the hot tub, which was still percolating in its constantly shifting lenses of color. "Wanna go for a dip?"

I turned back to look at him, but he had already dropped his boxers. I slipped down into the warm water, realizing how soothing it was to my tired muscles. I wasn't sure if they were tired from all the prep work for the party or from some of the more athletic positions Ryan had put me in when we'd gone for round two just an hour ago.

He wrapped his arm around me, pulling me to his

body. "So was that everything you ever hoped it would be and more?"

I shook my head, looking up at him to witness the shocked expression on his face. I am sure he thought it was a rhetorical question.

"This," I said, throwing my leg over him and climbing onto his lap, "this is everything I ever hoped it would be… and more."

"Valley, you are something else." He chuckled before pressing a kiss against my lips. "But I love you for it."

"Hey, you told me to make friends!" I reminded him.

"I guess I should be careful what I wish for," he quipped, pressing another kiss to my lips. "I think I'm going to like having this kind of friends, though."

"Me too," I agreed. "Even if having 'this kind of friends' only makes me love you that much more."

"I know a lot of people wouldn't understand it," he said, locking his eyes with mine. "But I think you're right."

"Of course I'm right!" I teased him. "I'm always right."

THE END

Read the next book of the Spice Up Our Marriage
Series here:
Rule Breaker

Join my readers group so you always know when the
next release will be:
www.facebook.com/groups/PhoebesAngels

ABOUT THE AUTHOR

USA Today Bestselling Author Phoebe Alexander writes sexpositive, bodypositive erotic romance featuring compelling plots intertwined with passionate, fiery encounters. She believes that real, relatable characters can have even steamier sex than billionaires, rock stars, and the young and lithe-bodied. She also advocates for ethical non-monogamy through her writing.

Phoebe lives on the East Coast of the US with her husband, sons, and multiple fur babies. When she's not writing, she works as an editor and consultant for indie authors. She also volunteers her time running a 5000-member indie author support group. Her sexual fantasies have all been fulfilled, and now her single greatest fantasy is just having some damn free time.

twitter.com/eroticphoebe
instagram.com/authorphoebealexander
amazon.com/Phoebe-Alexander/e/B00ANN43WK
bookbub.com/authors/phoebe-alexander

Loyalty & Lies

Alpha Bet Guys Series

A Hole

The Big O

Need the D

Hard F

Ride the C

Spice Up Our Marriage Series

Project Paradise

Rule Breaker

The Playground